*"My baby's father promised to marry me the next morning. Otherwise I never would have...you know..."*

Chin quivering, Emmaline brought her red-rimmed, dewy gaze to Johnny, her voice barely above a whisper. "I was...uh, saving myself. For my wedding night. If—of course—I was ever going to have a wedding of my own, which until that night seemed doubtful."

Johnny was a man conflicted. Part of him wanted to find the jerk who'd done this to her and pound him into a pulp, and part of him hoped the creep had disappeared for good. Emmaline was such a funny little thing. Stodgy as a toad, with the dreams of a fairy princess.

"I'm a science tutor!" she cried. "What will I tell my students? Or...or...the ladies in the ch-ch-*church choir!*"

Without preamble, and as calmly as if he were inviting her to the movies, Johnny found himself saying, "Marry me."

Dear Reader,

Compelling, emotionally charged stories featuring honorable heroes, strong heroines and the deeply rooted conflicts they must overcome to arrive at a happily-ever-after are what make a Silhouette Romance novel come alive. Look no further than this month's offerings for stories to sweep you away....

In *Johnny's Pregnant Bride,* the engaging continuation of Carolyn Zane's THE BRUBAKER BRIDES, an about-to-be-married cattle rancher honorably claims another woman—and another man's baby—as his own. This month's VIRGIN BRIDES title by Martha Shields shows that when *The Princess and the Cowboy* agree to a marriage of convenience, neither suspects the other's real identity...or how difficult *not* falling in love will be! In *Truly, Madly, Deeply,* Elizabeth August delivers a powerful transformation tale, in which a vulnerable woman finds her inner strength and outward beauty through the love of a tough-yet-tender single dad and his passel of kids.

*And Then He Kissed Me* by Teresa Southwick shows the romantic aftermath of a surprising kiss between best friends who'd been determined to stay that way. A runaway bride at a crossroads finds that *Weddings Do Come True* when the right man comes along in this uplifting novel by Cara Colter. And rounding out the month is Karen Rose Smith with a charming story whose title says it all: *Wishes, Waltzes and a Storybook Wedding.*

Enjoy this month's titles—and keep coming back to Romance, a series guaranteed to touch *every* woman's heart.

*Mary-Theresa Hussey*

Mary-Theresa Hussey
Senior Editor

Please address questions and book requests to:
Silhouette Reader Service
U.S.: 3010 Walden Ave., P.O. Box 1325, Buffalo, NY 14269
Canadian: P.O. Box 609, Fort Erie, Ont. L2A 5X3

# JOHNNY'S
# PREGNANT BRIDE

## Carolyn Zane

*Silhouette*
R O M A N C E™
Published by Silhouette Books
America's Publisher of Contemporary Romance

For my own little babies, Madeline and Olivia,
and their sweet father, Matt, who is the model for
the heroes in all of my books.
I love you all.
THANK YOU,
Dear Lord, for the laughter with which to face life's valleys.

 SILHOUETTE BOOKS

ISBN 0-373-19402-1

JOHNNY'S PREGNANT BRIDE

Visit us at www.romance.net

Printed in U.S.A.

## CAROLYN ZANE

lives with her husband, Matt, their preschool daughter Madeline and their latest addition, baby daughter Olivia, in the rolling countryside near Portland Oregon's Willamette River. Like Chevy Chase's character in the movie *Funny Farm*, Carolyn finally decided to trade in a decade of city dwelling and producing local television commercials for the quaint country life of a novelist. And even though they have bitten off decidedly more than they can chew in the remodeling of their hundred-plus-year-old farmhouse, life is somewhat saner for her than for poor Chevy. The neighbors are friendly, the mail carrier actually stops at the box and the dog, Bob Barker, sticks close to home.

# THE BRUBAKER FAMILY
## of Texas

Big Daddy - m. - Miss Clarise

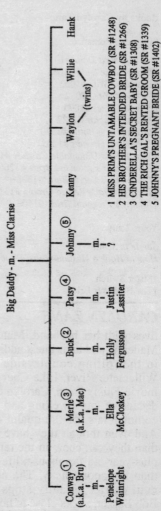

Conway ① (a.k.a. Bru)
—m.—
Penelope Wainright

Merle ③ (a.k.a. Mac)
—m.—
Ella McCloskey

Buck ②
—m.—
Holly Fergusson

Patsy ④
—m.—
Justin Lassiter

Johnny ⑤
—m.—
?

Kenny

Waylon

Willie
(twins)

Hank

1 MISS PRIM'S UNTAMABLE COWBOY (SR #1248)
2 HIS BROTHER'S INTENDED BRIDE (SR #1266)
3 CINDERELLA'S SECRET BABY (SR #1308)
4 THE RICH GAL'S RENTED GROOM (SR #1339)
5 JOHNNY'S PREGNANT BRIDE (SR #1402)

# Chapter One

Unable to breathe, Emmaline Arthur stared at her doctor, the very doctor that had delivered her, as if he'd lost a sizable chunk of his gray matter.

Pregnant.

Her, of all people.

Why…in the 9,230 or so days that Emmaline had lived on this planet, she'd only had one lone, brief encounter with the opposite sex. An encounter she'd just as soon forget. An encounter that certainly could not have left her in the family way.

Could it?

Her mind flashed back to the evening of her friend Nora's wedding reception, and a red-hot fire stole into her cheeks.

Stupid fool! Stupid, stupid fool!

The self-deprecating refrain now came automatically in the month that had passed since the wedding. It reverberated through her brain every time she thought of that humiliating night. She blinked and tried to shove the ugly memories out of her mind. That horrible event had nothing to do with Dr. Chase's diagnosis. No. Dr. Chase was simply wrong. He was getting up there in years. Close to retirement now. Mistake prone. She would get a second opinion.

Twenty-five years ago, Emmaline Marie Arthur had been born an overachiever, foregoing baby toys for the encyclopedia by the time she could pry the books off the shelf. The never-been-married research scientist at SystaMed Cancer Research Institute, former Girl Scout, paragon of virtue, only child of prominent and much-esteemed educators didn't know the meaning of the word *wild.* Unless, of course, one was speaking of a rogue cancer cell.

Certainly Dr. Chase knew that.

Heavens, everyone in the small town of Hidden Valley, Texas, knew that about the homely young girl who had graduated high school while Doogie Howser was still getting a handle on phonics. She'd then gone on to work on a host of degrees while all the other young girls her age were planning their coming-out parties. Parties to which she'd never been invited. Not to one.

She knew why. And she didn't care.

Beauty and phony social skills meant nothing to her. It was common knowledge that the studious, plain-as-lumpy-oatmeal Emmaline was not interested in frivolous social occasions. That she'd spent most of her youth studying, precluded any opportunity to date. Not that anyone would have looked twice at the freckle-faced, buck-toothed child prodigy with braces and headgear that could have picked up satellite signals. Not to mention the magnifying glasses that dominated her gamin face, enlarging the look of her eyes to frightening proportions.

And though her teeth were now straight and her body curved, nothing much else about Emmaline or her social life had changed. That is, until the wedding reception of her friend and co-worker, Nora.

Her tongue darted out to wet lips that had become dry with her shallow breathing.

"Dr. Chase, are you certain that you haven't made some mistake? Surely the test could tell you that I might be pregnant when I'm not." As a research scientist, Emmaline knew that mistakes could be made in the lab.

Dr. Chase smiled a knowing smile. A smile that said in his forty odd years of practice that he'd seen it all. Even the likes of a highly ethical, somewhat socially backward girl like Emmaline finding herself in the family way outside the marriage bed. "I performed the test twice, honey. You are most assuredly pregnant."

Johnny Brubaker couldn't breathe.

In fact, he felt as if he were dying.

Clamping his eyes tightly shut, he struggled to draw precious oxygen into his lungs and willed the waves of nausea to subside. As he passed a clammy hand over his fevered brow, he hoped he wasn't dying in the literal sense of the word.

Yet.

However, it sure as heck felt as if he had all the classic symptoms of imminent death. Thready pulse, profuse sweating, labored breathing and a definite sense that the Grim Reaper was lurking behind the lush velvet draperies that adorned the expansive windows in the Brubaker family library.

Clawing at his bolo tie, Johnny loosened the collar of his Western shirt and leaned back in his father's comfortable leather-upholstered wing back chair. His wild gaze roved the room and searched, unseeingly, for the answer to his current state of distress.

As ranch foreman here at the Circle BO, he'd been—only moments before—out in the south section with the other hands on his father's giant spread. And all morning he'd worked like a dog out in the blazing Texas sun and never felt better. Or more alive. Having just turned twenty-eight, he was finally hitting his stride mentally and physically. He was too young to simply keel over out of the blue.

Wasn't he?

It had only been since he'd joined his fiancée, Felicity Lowenstone, and his parents, Big Daddy and Miss Clarise in the Brubaker mansion's tastefully appointed, stunningly opulent library that he'd begun to feel so rotten. As their happy conversation swirled around him, he debated whether or not he should pick up the phone and demand the paramedics. Nah. He didn't want to jump the gun. Not for a little thing like a coronary thrombosis. If it got any worse than these crushing lung pains and fuzzy vision, then he'd call. In the meantime, he'd sit here, tough it out and try to gather his wits.

"And these—" Felicity handed a stack of RSVP cards to Miss Clarise "—are probably the last of the responses for the wedding and reception to come in. It's about time, considering the wedding is only five days away." She squealed with excitement.

Johnny's heart slammed against his ribs and then

took a full gainer with a half twist into his stomach. He clutched his chest. What in thunder was going on? For a moment he tried to remember when he'd last had his cholesterol checked.

Mouth open wide, pearly caps flashing, Felicity's nasal giggle brayed up and down the scales, leaving Johnny with the feeling that his rear molars had just been drilled without benefit of Novocain.

Criminy, he felt awful. High-strung. Edgy. Slowly, his eyes strayed over to his tastefully adorned, stunningly coifed fiancée.

Why had he never noticed what an abrasive laugh Felicity had before now? From time to time over the past year, his younger brothers would imitate her, but he'd always chalked that up to the fact that those idiots were just jealous. Perhaps his current "out of body" experience was helping him to see things a little more clearly. Because his brothers were right.

Felicity's laugh was annoying as hell.

"According to my calculations," Felicity gushed, displaying the guest list, computer-printed on what looked to Johnny like an endless ream of papers, "we should have nearly a thousand guests!" Again, her laughter scraped Johnny's sensitive eardrums like steel wool on a chalkboard. His head throbbed. He needed an aspirin. He needed a drink. No.

He needed an IV drip and a heart surgeon.

"Why, that's just wonderful, honey." Miss Clarise's well-modulated Southern drawl was a lovely counterbalance to Felicity's discordant squeals. Johnny's mother leaned forward and took the list from her daughter-in-law-to-be. "You've been working hard."

"Sure have, honey bunch!" Big Daddy crowed in

jubilation, thrilled with the idea of another huge Brubaker wedding. Especially one between the Lowenstone Corporation and the Brubaker dynasty. "Why y'all's weddin' is just the icing on our families' little merger. If this deal your daddy and I are cookin' up, to take over the failin' Magtron Oil, goes they way we think it should, your future and Johnny's—" he gestured grandly to his fifth offspring "—will be secure forever! Hot-diggity-dog, this calls for a celebration!" Leaping off his seat, Johnny's diminutive father strode to the bar and poured a round of drinks for everyone.

Twin spots as bright as molten lava stained Felicity's otherwise porcelain cheeks. "Oh, I'm just so happy for all of us! I know my own papa hasn't been this excited about a business deal in years. In fact, Big Daddy, my papa is finally coming out of the depression that has plagued him since he lost so much on the stock market last year. That's why I want this wedding to be extraspecial. For everyone."

"Well, you're doin' a bang-up job on the plannin' end, honey pie." Big Daddy tossed a wide, elastic grin over his shoulder.

Johnny's windpipe seemed to slam shut. His fingertips began to tingle.

Turning in her seat, Felicity smiled coquettishly at her fiancé. "It's been fun, really. I love to organize social events. I'd have a party every day, if I could!" Long false eyelashes fluttered against the two fiery patches that signaled her high level of zeal. "I can hardly wait for our wedding! I just know it will be the talk of the town for years!"

Johnny smiled weakly and tried to catch his breath. "Hmm." His *hmm* was noncommittal. It was all he could manage, considering his lips and tongue sud-

denly felt as if they belonged to someone else. Someone suffering from typhoid.

Wriggling with excitement, Felicity shuffled
through the stack of catalogs and order forms on her
lap. "Okay, okay, okay." She flapped her hands in
enthusiasm. "I called Monaco's department store this
morning? You know? A-a-and we have gotten almost
everything we've registered for at the bridal registry!
Isn't that simply divine?"

Felicity Lowenstone. The little woman. Soon to be
his better half. His soul mate, partner in life...lover.
Good grief. Swiping at the sweat that beaded his upper
lip with his tingling hand, he suddenly realized a fact
that had somehow managed to elude him for this past
year. It was happening. Really happening.

He was getting married.

And, by the look of things, it was too late to back
out. Sitting perfectly still, he tried to compose himself.
To sort out his feelings. Did he want to back out? Is
this why he was suddenly feeling so...so...claus-
trophobic? So out of control? So sick at heart?

So...doomed?

Was the fact that within five short days he was giving up his freedom killing him? No. He wasn't that
shallow. His freedom didn't mean all that much to him
in the scheme of things. Fact of the matter was, Johnny
was looking forward to becoming a husband and father. Especially a father. The idea of a bunch of kids
to toss in the air made him happy. For a moment he
pictured his future daughters, squealing with rather abrasive laughter, doe eyes, sticky lips pursed as they
checked their wedding gifts for brand names and de-
signer labels.

Realizations came fast and hard to Johnny Brubaker in those fleeting moments. He studied his future wife as she tugged her tailored skirt over her rail-thin thighs to better cover her knobby knees. Suddenly, things he'd been blinded to were becoming crystal clear. He was getting married to a woman he didn't love. In fact, he was getting married to a woman he didn't really even know.

His eyes roved over the expensive, well-put-together package that was Felicity Lowenstone and he suddenly had the feeling that she was all smoke and mirrors.

Who was this woman?

Okay, so they'd grown up together. But did they really know each other? The way a man and a woman who were pledging eternity to each other should know each other?

Extending a well-manicured hand, Felicity accepted the icy glass that Big Daddy offered and set it carefully on her coaster.

"Okay, listen, listen, listen. I have confirmations from all the hotels where we will be staying on our honeymoon." She handed copies to Miss Clarise. "A-a-and, here is a copy of our itinerary, just in case you need to get in touch with us over the next two months, you know? We should be able to call you back from the yacht on any day that does not have a star posted next to it." Holding the pages aloft, she went over her color-coded version of the impending honeymoon.

"What an interesting idea," Miss Clarise murmured, noting with some amazement the grids and time lines her son's fiancée had drawn to chart their every honeymoon move.

"Oh, I don't believe in being out of touch at any given moment." Felicity patted her well-sprayed hair as if daring it to disobey the complex confines set by her stylist. "Can't chance missing an important function or the latest bit of gossip."

The fickle fingers of fate tightened around Johnny's throat, completely cutting off his air supply as his future began to shrivel before his eyes.

He was not in love with Felicity.

Unfortunately along with this depressing realization came the knowledge that sooner rather than later he was going to have to fess up.

As she stood before the mansion's impressive entryway, Emmaline's fingertips hovered above the polished gold doorbell. For the millionth time in less than an hour, she wondered if she was doing the right thing. Well, to heck with the right thing, she finally decided with uncustomary vehemence. The time for doing the right thing was past.

Johnny Brubaker should have thought about the consequences of his irresponsible actions long before he showed up at Nora's wedding reception last month. It took two to tango, and she was only partly to blame for this mess. Giving the doorbell a vicious stab, Emmaline still couldn't believe how gullible she'd been. For heaven's sake, she hadn't even known the real name of her seducer until an hour ago. Luckily, Nora had been able to help her unwind the tangled mystery of Johnny Brubaker. When Emmaline had dialed her co-worker from her car phone while still in Dr. Chase's parking lot, she'd been unable to stem the tide of tears. When she was finally coherent, the whole sordid story poured out, and Nora was devastated for her friend.

"What did he look like, honey?"

Emmaline sighed a ragged sigh into the phone's mouthpiece. "Gorgeous. Far too gorgeous for me." She emitted a small, derisive laugh. "He was tall, dark and handsome, and had deep dimples in each cheek. And, there was something about him that was at once sophisticated and sort of cowboylike."

"And you say his name was Ronny Shumacher?" Nora sounded bewildered. "I don't know anyone by that name invited to our wedding. But the way you describe him sounds like Chuck's boss out at the Circle BO. You've been by there...you know, it's the giant white mansion about a half hour out of town. Anyway, Johnny Brubaker looks just like the guy you describe."

"So that's his real name."

"Yes, but he's a real sweetie pie. In fact, I think he's getting married next week himself. I'd be shocked if he would seduce anyone for money, or any reason, for that matter."

Exhaling deeply, Emmaline scribbled Johnny's name and the ranch's whereabouts on a scrap that she'd found in her purse. "Nora, at this point nothing would shock me anymore."

Nora tsked and hmmed for a moment, deep in thought. "You know, Johnny is the only man who fits your description that we invited to our wedding. But, as I think back, I don't remember seeing him there."

A most unladylike grunt came from deep within Emmaline's throat. "That's because he was otherwise occupied."

With that, she bid Nora an emotional goodbye and

set off for the infamous Circle BO. Within the hour,
her heart pounding a ragged drum solo in her ear, Emmaline stood before the threshold, ready to meet once
more the man that had fathered her unborn child.

As she leaned forward, her breath fogged the intricate,
leaded panes of glass that made up the window in the
giant, mahogany double entry door. She took a deep,
calming breath. She couldn't let the fact that these
people were fabulously wealthy cow her. This blankety-blank dirtbag owed her an audience and she
would have it come heck or high water.

Through the window the intimidating, massive
foyer seemed an endless sea of black-and-white marble squares. Pillars supported grand arches that led off
in any number of different directions. Rainbows from
the sparkling crystal chandeliers danced lazily on the
walls in the sunlight. The staircase alone would have
put *Gone with the Wind*'s Tara to shame. Never before
had Emmaline seen such opulence.

From where she stood on this huge antebellum mansion's front porch, Emmaline could see rows of pillars,
like sturdy sentinels, guarding the house proper, sup-
porting the huge second-floor verandah. The fantasti-
cally long driveway was lined with shade trees, and a
half dozen other buildings dotted the surrounding area.
Servants' quarters, a giant garage, the pool house, a
gazebo, a greenhouse and the stables. It was fearsome
to behold.

Although, it wasn't as if she were exactly poverty-
stricken herself. Her parents had given her a lovely,
middle-class upbringing and a fine education. She'd
had everything she'd ever needed and more. The simple fact that all three stories of her folks' entire house
could most likely fit in the foyer that sprawled beyond

the front door was no reason to get all panicky. No.
She had more than just herself to think of now. She
had a baby on the way.

Oh, merciful heavens, how on earth was she going
to tell her parents? Their faces, beaming with pride,
flashed before her eyes. Blinking away the image, she
gathered her determination before it failed her altogether and yet again prodded the dulcet tones from the
bell within. Emmaline held her breath and allowed her
feelings of impotent rage to take over once more. Beyond the glass she could see a member of the staff
moving across the expansive foyer to greet her. Too
late to back out now. Well that was fine and dandy.

Emmaline knew she had nothing to be ashamed of.
She'd been more victim in this debacle than perpetrator. She guessed.

Anyway, she had rights.

She was a woman on a mission. Here to kick some
rich playboy tail. No high-society Lothario was going
to take advantage of Emmaline Arthur.

Saved by the bell.

The clichéd phrase echoed through Johnny's mind
as he shrugged and shook his head. He'd been on the
verge of spilling his guts to Felicity. Had he spoken a
moment sooner, he'd have been able to excuse himself
and his fiancée from the library for a much-needed
break.

Then, maybe as they strolled among the rose gar-
dens that were blooming in full splendor, he could
confide his concerns in Felicity. In private. She would
understand. She would be glad, in the long run. Once
she came to terms with the shock, she would be relieved to discover his feelings—or lack thereof—be-

fore the wedding took place. Unfortunately that would have to wait.

One of the day butlers popped his balding pate into the library. "There is a lady here who wishes to discuss business with Mr. Johnny Brubaker. She is waiting in the foyer."

Big Daddy paused in his perusal of the lengthy wedding guest list long enough to glance up at the butler and then frown at his son, who was only too happy to make good his escape for some fresh air.

"Tell her he's busy makin' his weddin' plans. Get a callin' card and tell her he'll get back to her later." Big Daddy nodded deferentially to Felicity. "Dad-blamed salespeople. We are plagued by door-to-door types prit'near every day."

Felicity nodded in total sympathy.

"Yes, sir." The butler disappeared.

"Calling card?"

Johnny frowned as the disgruntled saleswoman's shriek echoed throughout the foyer and into the library.

"You want a calling card? Here's a calling card for you to give that blankety-blank Johnny Brubaker! You tell him to get out here and take his lumps like a man!"

The butler remained unflappable. "And, may I inquire as to precisely why, madam?"

Her voice escalating, their visitor's words reached the little group with shocking clarity. "Not that it's any of your business, but that Johnny Brubaker creep got me pregnant and left me holding the bag, that's why!"

# Chapter Two

Everyone turned to stare at Johnny, as the voice from the entryway reverberated through the house.

An inarticulate cry squeaked past Felicity's slack lips, as a sheaf of sales receipts slipped from her brightly lacquered fingertips and floated to the floor. She lifted her spiky lashes to him, beseeching him to tell her it wasn't so.

Rising to his feet, Johnny scowled, trying to make sense of the foreign words this woman in the foyer was shouting.

What?

Pregnant?

By him?

No way. What kind of a scam was this? He'd heard of women claiming to be pregnant by wealthy men before, but he never thought it would happen to him. He'd always avoided that kind of a trap like the plague.

Jaw grim with determination, Johnny strode across

the library floor toward the door. He'd handle this before it got out of control.

"Hold on there, son." Big Daddy trotted across the room and put a restraining hand on Johnny's arm.

Plowing his fingers through his hair in frustration, Johnny looked down at the tiny patriarch of the enormous Brubaker clan, as the older man clung to his bicep. He shook off his father's arm.

"I can take care of this, Big Daddy."

"Not yet." The old man's eyes were narrowed with suspicion, whether for his son's behavior or this stranger's accusations, Johnny couldn't be sure. "You don't want to go off half-cocked now, that's how ya end up gettin' sued. This situation—" he thumped his Stetson back with a stubby thumb "—requires a cool head. Let me go find out what she wants. You stay here and reassure your little gal and your mama that everything's gonna be okay. I'll come and gitcha in a minute and you can set the record straight with this woman."

His gaze shooting to his mother and fiancée, Johnny could see their shock and pain.

Ah, bloody hell, this was definitely not his day.

He glanced at his father. As much as he hated to admit it, Big Daddy made sense.

"All right."

He would capitulate. For a few minutes. But once he'd organized his thoughts, he was going to go out there and read this woman the riot act. He had rights. No gold-digging opportunist was going to blackmail him. Especially for something he didn't do.

Big Daddy disappeared into the foyer, and Johnny turned to face the women. They were obviously stricken by this charade going on out in the foyer. The

wounded look in his mother's eyes pierced his heart.
And poor Felicity rattled like a skeleton in the breeze.

"Johnny? Honey?" Voice thready, bony arms extended, Felicity's fingertips fluttered toward him, and she looked as if she were about to fall over. "What's going on?"

Crossing quickly over to the women, Johnny assisted them back into their seats and attempted to explain something he did not himself understand.

"I'm not sure, but I think—"

Before he could continue, Big Daddy burst back into the room. Face a brilliant shade of crimson, the older man eyeballed his son, his cool head quite obviously a thing of the past. "Some little gal goes by the name of Emmaline Arthur claims you put her in the family way last month. That right?"

Johnny stood and faced his father. "No." A muscle jerked in his jaw.

Clearly, Big Daddy was not convinced. "She's got your name and described you to a tee, boy. Said she met you at Chuck's weddin'."

"Chuck, our ranch hand?" Johnny remembered being invited to the wedding, but he'd had other plans that weekend.

"Yup. You better get out there and figure this mess out. Then, come back in here. You've got some fancy explainin' to do."

Felicity began to weep in earnest, her mouth contorted, her false lashes scrunched shut, blackish tears flowing down her gaunt cheeks. Groping into her purse, she located a handkerchief and trumpeted into the lacy scrap.

Miss Clarise put a consoling arm around the young

woman's frail shoulders. "There, there," she murmured.

With a last apologetic look at the trio, Johnny strode into the foyer to meet his fate.

Emmaline took one look at the tall, dark and handsome man that stalked like an angry animal toward her from across the foyer and knew she'd made a terrible mistake. Her eyes welled and her throat closed.

"You're not Johnny Brubaker." Mortified, she could barely choke out the words.

The dark thundercloud that had accompanied him into the massive entryway began to dissipate as she stared at him in shock.

Quite obviously this was not the same man she'd met at the wedding. Little stars floated before her eyes. Light-headed, she blinked at him and tried to reconcile this new bit of information with the rest of the devastating news she'd received that day.

"Don't tell that to my mama, she thinks I'm the real thing." His tone was dry, but a grudging grin tipped the corner of his sculpted mouth.

"I...I don't know what to say. I don't... understand." Emmaline felt the familiar bile of nausea rise and knew at once she was going to be sick.

Oh, perfect. Just great.

It was bad enough to walk into a complete stranger's home and accuse him of fathering her child out of wedlock, but now she was going to disgrace herself even further. Her eyes darted about and landed on a giant potted palm near the foot of the staircase. Rushing across the marble tiles, she reached it just in time to retch violently into the terra-cotta container.

Coughing and sputtering among the fronds, she hid her head and wished for a meteorite to sweep through the foyer and blow her into oblivion. Luckily she was getting pretty good at this throwing up business. She fumbled in her pocket, located the tissues she carried for just such an occasion and proceeded to mop her brow and tidy her lips.

A firm hand at the back of her neck was cool and calming.

"You going to be okay?" There was a real concern in the low, velvety tones.

"Oh, sure." She tried to don a breezy, unaffected attitude. "Although I can't speak for your plant..." When she stood upright, she wasn't quite so confident. Beads of sweat popped out on her forehead, and she felt positively green.

"You don't look so good. Come into the parlor with me, and you can sit for a spell. You look as if you could use something to drink."

"That would be nice."

As docilely as a puppy, Emmaline followed Johnny into the elegant, empty parlor and allowed herself to be settled into a comfortable, overstuffed couch. With the touch of a button, the footrest popped up, and Emmaline found herself reclining in a room that surely rivaled heaven's most tasteful decor.

The Texas afternoon sunshine streamed through the floor-to-ceiling windows, casting an ethereal glow about the room, setting the crystal objets d'art on fire and causing the silver and gold accent pieces to sparkle. Lovely marble statues were positioned between the windows, and the long, gauzy white curtains puddled richly on the mahogany floor and billowed in the slight country breezes.

Emmaline watched as Johnny prepared her an icy sparkling water with a twist of lemon at the wet bar in the corner. He certainly fit the basic physical description of the dandy she'd met at Nora's wedding, but this Johnny was far more rugged. Earthy. Obviously used to working outdoors. And working hard, if the muscles that bulged beneath his formfitting Western shirt were any indication. And his dimples were deeper and even more adorable than Ronny's.

No, this man was clearly not the father of her baby. And if he wasn't, then who was? Nora didn't know anyone named Ronny Shumacher. Her shoulders sagged. She'd been so certain that she had the right man.

"Here you go." Johnny held out a drink as he ambled up beside her. "This should help settle your stomach. My sister used to swear by it, when she was pregnant with her daughter, Crystal Gayle."

Emmaline frowned. "Your sister is Crystal Gayle's mother?" Gracious. She really was out of her league. Struggling, she attempted to force her footrest down with her feet. She had to get out of here.

He motioned for her to stay where she was. "Yes, Crystal Gayle the preschooler, not the singer." His grin was dazzling. "In our family we're all named after country-western stars. It's a Brubaker tradition. I'm named for Johnny Cash."

"Oh." Emmaline smiled weakly, diverted for a moment. She took several sips of the sparkling water.

"Better?"

"Some." She nodded.

"Good. Sit here for a while, until you get your sea legs."

Johnny took the seat beside her on the couch and

attempted to put her at ease with some small talk. Considering her face was still clammy and no doubt the color of chalk, she was grateful he didn't expect her to explain immediately.

"My dad, Big Daddy Brubaker named all nine of us after his favorites. My oldest brother is Conway, but we call him Bru. Then, after Bru comes Merle, who goes by Mac, then there's Buck, Patsy, me, Kenny, the twins Waylon and Willie, and last but not least, Hank."

Emmaline was silent for a moment, wondering how it must have been to be raised in the middle of such a large family. Having been an only—and quite doted-upon—child, she couldn't begin to relate.

"Any of your brothers look like you?" she wondered aloud, grasping at one last straw.

"Not much. Maybe someday Hank will, but he's still a growing boy."

Tears pricked the backs of Emmaline's eyes, and she sighed. "I'm so sorry." Her throat constricted with embarrassment and confusion. As she glanced at the crystal glass she held in her hands, the tears welled, then spilled over her lower lashes and rolled down her cheeks to splash into her lap. "I've...I've made a terrible mistake by...coming here today. I shouldn't have bothered you." Lip quivering, chin trembling, she cast a watery smile at him.

"Hey, don't. I wasn't doing anything all that important." His smile was truly sympathetic.

An impatient knock sounded at the parlor door.

"Excuse me," Johnny murmured, patting her hand.

"Mmm." Emmaline plucked a dry tissue from her suit jacket pocket and tried to stem the tide that his kindness had brought on, but it was useless. Hormones and humiliation were a lethal combination, and Emmaline prided herself on not being an emotional sort. Ohhh. She sniffed and dabbed at her glasses. Her whole life was upside down.

Johnny strode across the parlor and pulled open the door to find his father peering curiously into the room.

"What's goin' on?" On tiptoe, the old man strained to see over his son's broad shoulder. "We've been waitin' in there on pins and needles, son."

Johnny sighed his impatience. It was obvious to him that the pathetic little waif that sat behind him on the couch was in trouble. Deep trouble. Couldn't his family see that? Couldn't Felicity tough it out for a few simple minutes? Irritated, Johnny watched his father hop from one foot to the other to get a better look at the woman who had claimed to carry his latest grandchild.

Willing himself to be patient, he rubbed the muscles at the back of his neck and stepped protectively into the doorway to block his father's view. "I know, but this is going to take a while. I'm sorry, Big Daddy, but you are just going to have to wait until I get this all sorted out. I'll come give you all a report just as soon as we're finished."

"Bu-but..." Big Daddy sputtered as Johnny shut the door in his father's face.

Slowly Johnny turned toward Emmaline and his heart went out to her. Something about the crooked parting and the spiky bangs in her ruler-straight, no-frills hairdo reminded him of a little kid who'd chopped her ponytail off just above her shoulders, in a fit of whimsy. And the heavy tortoiseshell framed glasses she wore, perched on her delicate nose, only added to her owlish looks. Her suit was nondescript and bulky in its lines, and her shoes were downright unflattering. Under other circumstances she might have appeared formidable. Studious. No-nonsense.

However, sitting here in tears and attempting to find the father of her unborn child, she only looked lost and dazed.

Johnny couldn't put his finger on it, exactly, but something about this little stranger brought out a protective streak in him as wide as the Lone Star state. Made him feel strong and big and manly. Things he usually never felt with Felicity. Ambling back over to the couch, he sat down beside her.

"Sorry about the interruption."

"Oh, that's okay." Waiving a soggy tissue, she attempted to smile at him through her tears.

Her glasses had fogged, endearing her even further to Johnny. She was a mess.

"You, uh—" he cleared his throat "—you want to tell me what you're doing here?"

With a meek nod, Emmaline hiccuped and set her glass on the end table's marble top. Pushing with her chunky open-toed sling-backs, she struggled to bring the footrest down so that she could sit up straight.

"Of course," she puffed, feet flailing, "I owe you an explanation for the way I came…barging in here…like some kind of deranged maniac. I assure you—"

"Here…" Johnny tried to stifle a grin at her ungainly attempts to sit up. "Allow me."

He reached across her body and touched a button that had her springing against him in a full, upright position. As she jostled about, he steadied her shoulders and upper arms with his hands. He couldn't help but admire the sturdy feel of her body beneath his fingertips. And, he couldn't help but compare. Felicity's shoulders were pointed as Egyptian pyramids.

"Oh." Emmaline clutched at her suit jacket and shrank away from him. "Uh, thank you." She squinted up at his face, then down at the hands that still rested against her shoulders. A hot blush crawled up her neck and ignited the pallid tone of her cheeks.

"No problem." Johnny sat back and propped his arms on his knees, letting his hands dangle between his legs. He nodded at her. "Go on, please."

"Yes, of course. Now then…" She shook her head, as if to clear it. "Oh, yes. I simply wanted to assure you that I don't make a habit out of barging into other people's homes, accusing them of…of…"

"Getting you pregnant and leaving you holding the bag," Johnny quoted. Deliberately he kept his tone light. "I believe you."

"You do?"

Nodding, his expression was sage. "Yes."

"Oh, thank you. Thank you." She twisted in her seat and regarded him through the tears that hovered against her lower lashes. "Honestly, I don't know how any of this happened to me. I mean, I still can't believe it's true." As she blubbered she wrapped her tissue so tightly around her finger its tip began to turn blue.

With a frown, Johnny took her hand in his, unwound the tissue and rubbed her fingertip. "Are you sure you want to talk about it?"

Emmaline shook her head. "No." She sobbed another hiccup. "Yes." She shrugged and cast a baleful look up at him. "I don't know."

"Why don't you start by telling me why you came to see me."

Lashes lowered, she spoke haltingly. "After the

doctor told me I was pregnant this afternoon, I knew I owed the father of my baby the truth. No matter what kind of a reptile he is.'' She darted a defiant glance at him.

"I gather that you haven't known the father long?" Startled by his blunt question, Emmaline's face crumpled. "I only knew him for that one night."

A one-night stand? Johnny arched a curious brow. She hardly seemed the type.

As if she sensed his surprise, Emmaline took a deep breath and began to pour out the entire story.

"Actually, I met him at Chuck and Nora's wedding—"

"Chuck Fargo, my ranch hand?"

"Uh-huh. Nora said they'd invited you?"

"Yes, but I was out of town that weekend."

"Oh." Emmaline released a slow sigh. "Well, anyway, I went to the wedding and met a guy who looks a lot like you. I thought he said his name was Ronny Shumacher, but when I called Nora she said she didn't know anyone by that name. Then, I described him to her and she thought maybe I was looking for Johnny Brubaker." Again the color in her cheeks heightened as she looked up at him. "I don't usually drink champagne, so I figured that I must have remembered his name wrong."

Johnny stared at her for a long moment.

Emmaline cleared her throat. "And, after talking it over with Nora, I thought for sure that you were him."

"The father of your baby?"

"Yes. It's uncanny how much you look like him. However, now that I'm here, I can easily see that you are not that much alike. True, you're both tall with dark hair and the same handsome facial features. Only, in person he...he seemed—'' her brow furrowed as she attempted to conjure his image ''—well, now that I look back, I can more clearly see that he probably wasn't as genuine as I wanted to believe. He was obviously an advantage taker.''

"If the bride and groom didn't know him, why was he there?" Johnny wondered aloud. Pulling a boot-clad ankle up over his knee, he sat back, giving her predicament his entire attention.

Emmaline lifted and dropped a shoulder. "Excellent question. I'm ashamed to admit I don't know the answer. Maybe he and his buddies heard the music echoing out of the hotel ballroom and come in from the bar across the lobby. Party crashers. He was probably from out of town." She drew her trembling lip between her teeth for a moment, to still it. "My baby's father is a party crasher. Just a no-account, blankety-blank reprobate party crasher."

Johnny admired her spunk. And the goofy way she cussed was cute as all get-out, too.

"I know this sounds childish and gullible, but he promised to marry me the next morning. Otherwise I never would have...you know..." Chin quivering, she brought her red-rimmed, dewy gaze to Johnny, her voice barely above a humiliated whisper. "I was...uh, saving myself. For my wedding night." A self-deprecating expression passed over her face. "If—of course—I was ever going to have a wedding of my own, which until that night seemed doubtful. But now, for all intents and purposes, my wedding night is over. And it was miserable! Nothing like I'd imagined."

With a strangled wail, she buried her head in her hands and sobbed her grief. "This has really not been my day."

Johnny could relate.

"I'm a science tutor! What will I tell my students? Or the other scientists at SystaMed? Or...or—" spasms grabbed and shook her entire body "—the ladies in the ch-ch-church choir!"

Johnny was a man conflicted. Part of him wanted to find the jerk who'd done this to her and pound him into a pulp, and part of him hoped the creep had disappeared for good. She was such a funny little thing. Stodgy as a toad, with the dreams of a fairy princess.

Tentatively, he reached out to put his arm around her shoulders. Before he knew it, she'd slumped into his embrace and was clutching his shirt, snuffling into the folds of fabric.

"The whole town will know! I have a fine reputation in the scientific field to protect. The people who fund our research down at SystaMed are very strict about our behavior both inside and outside the lab. They want only the best. The brightest. Does that sound like someone who would get herself knocked up by a perfect stranger? The ramifications are—" her eyes glazed over as these very ramifications began to hit home "—mind-boggling."

Johnny tucked the top of her head under his chin and stroked her dull brown hair. It was surprisingly silky and soft, unlike the sprayed and pinned helmet that Felicity wore.

"H-h-how am I going to face my parents?" Her wails were muffled by the folds of his shirt. "How am I going to tell them this news? It will kill them!"

"I know you don't want to hurt them." He did know. He had the same worries when it came to breaking the news to his own folks about calling off his wedding to Felicity. Disappointing parents who were proud of you, who believed in you, was never an easy task. "Do…uh, do you want to try and find the baby's father? I'm sure I could help. In the past my brother Mac has used the services of a very good private investigator—"

Emmaline shook her head. "Considering I don't even know where he's from, or anything about him—other than the fact that he looks like you—I don't see how finding him would be possible. I can't afford a manhunt, and I won't ask my folks for the money."

As much as Johnny hated to admit it, she was probably right. A few fuzzy memories and a name that may or may not have been his real name, was not much to go on, even for the top-of-the-line P.I. Of course, it could be done, but it would take time. And money. Didn't sound like she was too well fixed, financially speaking.

Emmaline attempted to smooth his damp and wrinkled shirt and at the same time compose herself. "Thank you just the same for your generous offer to connect me with an investigator, but no, thank you. You've done more than enough by simply sitting here and listening to me. I usually never bare my soul this way to anyone. I—" she scrubbed at her face with her tissue and forced a tremulous smile through her depression "—don't know what came over me. Must be hormones. You've been very nice and understanding. I've taken quite enough of your time."

"You're sure now, that you don't want to find him?"

Emmaline removed her glasses and ground at her eyes with the damp little ball of tissue and sighed. "Not anymore. I thought it was a good idea at first. But the more I think it over, the more I…well, I don't think I could live through confronting another man this way. Unless—'' her shy gaze flitted to his ''—he was as nice as you. And somehow, I doubt that.'' She waved her glasses about. ''I don't know him, and I'm thinking now that maybe I'd prefer to keep it that way. Anyone who would take advantage of a situation in this manner is not someone who would ever care about me or the baby. He made that perfectly clear the next morning, when he rescinded his marriage proposal.''

Yeah. Johnny had the sinking feeling that she was right. The guy who'd knocked her up wasn't someone she could trust.

He studied her gamin face, still splotchy and red from crying. Actually, once she'd taken off those hideous specs, he found that, much to his surprise, she wasn't as unattractive as he'd originally thought. Her eyes, almond shaped and wide set were lovelier than they looked behind the glasses, and the color was a rich hazel. In fact, all of her features, from her button nose to the bow of her lips were relatively classic and nicely arranged. If it weren't for her puffy eyes and red nose, and that horrible hairstyle that looked as if it had been styled by a hay thrasher without a driver, she'd be reasonably nice-looking.

With one swift move, she pushed her glasses back onto her face, and this illusion was curtained once more.

He squeezed his eyes shut hard, then opened them, bringing Emmaline's alter ego back into focus. ''What do you plan to do about the baby?''

''Why, raise it, of course.'' Spine stiffening, she answered the question as if there were no doubt. ''I have never shirked from responsibility, no matter what the consequences. My main concern is how my folks will react. They may disown me. But, that is a bridge I will have to cross when I get there. I have a good job—unless SystaMed decides to disown me as well. I'm over twenty-one, I...I can take care of myself and my...my...baby." Only the fear that flashed in her eyes belied the self-assurance of her words.

Johnny was once more moved by her internal fortitude. He wondered if she'd thought through the myriad problems of a future as a single parent, but the fact that she was willing to try touched him. He doubted that Felicity could ever weather such a storm.

Again there came a knock at the parlor door.

A deep sigh escaped his lips as Johnny stood. "Excuse me."

Emmaline nodded. "Of course."

He strode across the room, and once more Johnny found his father behind the door, straining to catch a glimpse of Emmaline.

"We need an answer in there, boy!" Big Daddy's anxious shout filled the air. "Felicity is nigh-on catatonic by now. What's goin' on? Is this little gal really pregnant?"

Johnny nodded.

"You gonna do the right thing?"

Johnny stared at his father, contemplating this question until he felt as if he'd been suddenly struck by lightning. Thunder crashed, ideas flashed, and Johnny Brubaker knew, as he peered back at the frumpy little research scientist that sat hunched on the couch, that up till now he'd been a drowning man.

That is, until he'd been thrown a lifeline in the form of one pregnant Emmaline Arthur.

"Yes." Solemnly he turned to regard his stricken

father. "I plan to do the right thing. For everyone involved. Now, please give me a little more time to figure out the logistics of our future, and then I'll come
explain everything."

# Chapter Three

As she waited for Johnny to finish speaking with his father, thoughts about that fateful night of Nora's wedding flitted through Emmaline's brain. She squeezed her eyes shut and tried to block the images that tortured, but it was impossible.

Since it had been a special occasion, Emmaline had allowed herself to indulge in a glass of champagne, knowing full well what it could do to her precious brain cells. Eventually she'd warmed up enough to mingle with the guests and soon found herself having fun.

The feeling was unique. Never had she felt quite so carefree. So happy for her good friend, Nora. Even though she was quite sure that Nora was making a huge mistake by marrying a man who was so obviously wrong for her. Nora was a brilliant scientist. Her fiancé, Chuck, was a simple ranch hand.

Emmaline doubted that love, no matter how strong,

could keep such opposites together. Ah, well. Luckily, she had no such illusions about love.

Nevertheless, she managed to get into the spirit of the occasion. She'd laughed, she'd mingled with a few senior citizens at her table and, amazingly enough, she'd danced, albeit awkwardly, with a partner, for the first time in her life. Beginning with the aged Mr. Healy, she'd been passed from septuagenarian to octogenarian and then, by some twist of fate, ended up with a young man she'd never met.

The handsome face of her seducer loomed up in her mind's eye, smiling, winking, flattering with his shallow praise. And she, so starved for attention, had drunk it up like the fine champagne that flowed from the fountain. He'd been extremely good-looking. So good-looking in fact, that she'd been quite shocked when he'd ambled across the room—breaking away from his hooting and catcalling buddies—and tapped on old Mr. Webster's stooped shoulder. For Emmaline it was love at first sight.

At long last, someone to whom physical beauty seemed inconsequential. Someone who appreciated her for her brilliance. For her ability to contribute to the welfare of society.

Ronny Shumacher.

Her soul mate.

Until that moment Emmaline had been saving herself for Mr. Right-Brain. Mr. Mensa. Mr. All-Brains-and-No-Brawn. She had no interest in a run-of-the-mill marriage, based on something as intangible as love. No. She was saving herself for companionship, common interest, trust. Saving herself for a night of…well, if not wedded bliss, than at least not revulsion, when the right time came.

But, hallelujah, she could forget all that because he'd arrived. Everything she'd ever dreamed of and tall, dark and handsome as all get-out to boot. She couldn't believe her luck. Silky smooth as fine chocolate, his flirtatious voice echoed in her mind.

"So, what's a bright woman like you doing without a date? I'd think the men would be knocking down your door to escort a sharp cookie like you to this wedding." And the clincher? "Tell me about your research."

Listening attentively, he'd kept the compliments and champagne flowing so that soon Emmaline's head was spinning with giddy joy. Little did she know that, at the moment he was sweet-talking her right off her feet, some of his buddies across the room had a hefty wager as to whether Mr. Ronny Shumacher could seduce the town virgin.

This unfortunate fact, she did not discover until the next morning.

It had taken a phenomenal amount of finesse, and obvious experience on his part, Emmaline had to admit as she thought back. However he was patient and eventually successful. Although, not without the promise of elopement, first thing in the morning. Even as she was swept off her feet, Emmaline attempted to adhere to her basic morals and core beliefs. Commitment was of utmost importance. Too bad her fuzzy brain had allowed the cart to pull ahead of the horse. That was so completely unlike her. Unfortunately, the morning arrived only to find Emmaline deflowered and her lover, the too-good-to-be-true Ronny Shumacher, sneaking out the door.

She couldn't seem to relive that night in the hotel room above the wedding reception, without Ronny's hurtful parting words from early the next morning, ringing in her ears.

"Marry you? Are you kidding?" He'd shrugged into his shirt, buckled his belt and snorted in derision. "No way, sweetheart. I've won the bet. Conquered the town virgin."

He stuffed his wallet and keys into his pockets as he stared down at her where she still lay on the bed, engulfed in humiliation. Waving off her protests and reminders of his promises, he interrupted.

"Listen, honey. I have no intention of marrying anyone, let alone someone as pitifully inexperienced and—" he paused, his eyes raking her over "—as physically and socially dull as you. I doubt that a spinster like you could ever satisfy a real man." Again, he snorted, then with a mocking salute, was gone.

The pain, however, remained.

Funny how amazingly easy it had been for him to seduce her, considering how right he'd been about her lack of sexual prowess. The baser instincts were not Emmaline's bag. Now, whisper sweet nothings in her ear about one of the three hundred substances that may inhibit angiogenesis, and she might begin to tingle and sweat.

No doubt he'd been well paid for his efforts. He and his buddies were probably still laughing up their sleeves at how the homely research scientist had kicked up her heels with a man so obviously out of her league. Well now, that would teach her, wouldn't it? Let down your guard for even a moment, and look what happens.

Emmaline shook her head, resolving to drive Ronny from her mind yet again. Removing her weighty glasses, she rubbed her eyes and chanced a blurry peek at Johnny's broad, muscular back. He was still speaking quite heatedly with his father.

A guilty grimace pinched her face. She was causing problems in his family. She should leave. Emmaline donned her glasses and prepared to go as Johnny closed the door, moved back across the room and sat down beside her once more. He seemed like such a wonderful man. Too bad he wasn't the man she'd met at the reception. Had he been, she felt sure she wouldn't be in this predicament now. He was a good guy, clearly raised on the same moral fiber for breakfast, lunch and dinner that she had been.

Something about Johnny Brubaker made her feel that she could sit here all day and bend his ear about her woes and not feel ashamed. However, she was beginning to wear out her welcome. He was needed elsewhere by his father. With a ragged exhalation, she straightened her jacket and moved to the edge of her seat.

It was time to go. Time to put together the shattered pieces and get on with what was left of her life. Touching her lips with the tip of her tongue, she angled her head to him and attempted to put into words the gratitude she felt.

"I have to be going now, but before I do, I just want to thank you for—"

"No."

Johnny reached out and clasped both her hands in his warm grasp. Emmaline could feel the calluses that spoke of hard work slightly abrading her own soft skin. Odd, such rough hands on such a rich man, she reflected. The incongruence was somehow appealing.

"No?"

"Please. Stay. I have an option I'd like you to consider regarding your predicament."

His face was so earnest, so compassionate, Emmaline knew for certain that he would never be the type of man to take advantage of a woman the way that Johnny or Ronny What's-His-Name at the wedding reception had.

"An option?" Emmaline shrugged. "What do you have in mind?"

Without preamble, and as calmly as if he were asking her to the movies, he spoke. "Marry me."

Johnny bit back a smile at the look of sheer revulsion that crossed Emmaline's face. He'd elicited many responses from many women in his life. However, such unmitigated disgust had never been one. Springing to his feet, he grabbed her glass and moved to the wet bar to refill it with sparkling water.

"Please, don't go until you've heard me out." He tossed a pleading look over his shoulder as he quickly raided the ice bucket. It was a good plan. If only he could make her see the beauty.

Johnny's mind flashed back to the wedding plans that Felicity had been making. He wasn't in love with Felicity.

And this unfortunate realization was becoming increasingly clear with each unfolding plan of the three-ring circus that was to be his mid-June wedding next Saturday afternoon. From the swans in the moat to the heart-shaped Milar balloons to be released into the azure Texas sky, Johnny knew in his soul that he had to call this charade off.

But how? Now that was the sixty-four-thousand dollar question. He glanced at Emmaline as his plan began to gel.

The wedding wheels were in motion. The guests had booked airfare. The gardeners were working overtime. The soloist had taken time off her national tour.

And here he was, the rotten SOB that had to go and realize that he didn't love Felicity just five short days before the wedding.

He liked good ol' Felicity just fine, as old family friends go, aside from her air raid siren of a laugh. But he didn't love her.

Why hadn't he noticed this before now? Oh, he loved the idea of loving Felicity. Of making his father happy by uniting their two business-compatible families in holy matrimony. Of seeing Magtron Oil flourish and provide jobs under the capable touch of their fathers. Of settling down and having a son to call his own.

His mind a million miles away, the sparkling water flowed over the rim of the glass. He cursed under his breath, then tossed Emmaline a sheepish glance. Water sloshing, he rushed her glass back to her and thrust it into her hand.

Now, if he could just convince a perfect stranger that she had to marry him. He fought back a wave of self-loathing and settled in next to Emmaline. How the devil had he let this happen? Although, why he should find the fact that he didn't love Felicity so startling was beyond him. Now that he stopped to analyze, Johnny knew that he'd never really been in love.

With anyone.

No. Johnny Brubaker wouldn't know true love if it came up and bit him in the butt.

He had to get out of this mess as quickly and as cleanly as possible. As he peered into Emmaline's ashen face, he knew that as escape routes went, she was his only option.

Brow wrinkled in fear and consternation, Emmaline contemplated his bizarre request. Perhaps she was no good at judging human character at all. First the gigolo at the wedding and now this guy? What kind of a wacko was he? Nobody proposed to a pregnant woman mere moments after meeting her. Especially one like Emmaline. At twenty-five years of age and having never been seriously kissed—that she could remember, anyway—she was under no illusions about her lack of allure to the opposite sex. And now suddenly this man wanted to marry her? Slowly she extracted her hands from his grasp.

"Pardon?" The single word was, at the moment, all she was able to squeak past the shock that shut her throat. She fumbled for her purse and made ready to leave. Heavens to Betsy, this was definitely not her day. "I thought Nora told me you were already engaged to be married. Soon."

Johnny passed a hand over his face and stared at her for a moment before he spoke. His mind was obviously whirring.

"I know this is sudden. And kind of crazy for a business proposition. But please, hear me out."

Gaze lowered, Emmaline fidgeted with her purse strap. She really did not want to hear this. However, he'd gone above and beyond the call of duty in listening to her humiliating story. She supposed sitting here, hearing him out for a few more minutes was the least she could do. After all, he didn't seem dangerous. Simply strange.

She squinted up at him. "You want to marry me?

As a business proposition?'' Her life just kept getting more bizarre by the moment.

"Yes." As his enthusiasm built, so did the speed and tenor of his voice. "Not like a regular marriage, based on love, of course." He waved the word aside as if it were simply a pesky irritant. "This would be a marriage of convenience. In name only. Strictly words on paper. And the marriage wouldn't have to last long at all. We could figure out when we are going to end it before we take the vows."

"Why on earth would you want to marry me? We've only just met!" She stared suspiciously at him, although she don't know why this absurd request surprised her at all. Nothing in her life made any sense anymore.

"Because the way I see it, we need each other."

Jaw slack, Emmaline stared at him, wondering if he'd just now gone daft or if he'd been born that way. "Okay. I can see why I might need you. But vice versa? No way. You need an expecting bride from the middle class, the way I need a dance with a party crasher. Besides, what will your fiancée think?"

"Yeah, right. Okay. I know it sounds nuts. But just hear me out, all right?" He ran a hand through his dark hair in a gesture Emmaline was beginning to recognize as habit. "I have a situation... No, let me rephrase. I don't want..." He stopped talking and cast a baleful glance at her.

"Aw, hell. You're right. I'm engaged. To a woman I don't love. The wedding is planned down to the monogrammed toothpicks and happening this Saturday. And just minutes before you stormed into my life, I came to the unfortunate realization that I—" his cheeks puffed as he exhaled tiredly "—I have never loved her."

"Not at all?"

He shook his head, looking genuinely remorseful.

Had she heard his confession before today, Emmaline might not have felt a bit of sympathy for his plight. Poor privileged boy unhappily engaged. But now... Well now she was busy developing compassion for all kinds of people who suddenly found themselves in trouble. She was beginning to realize that sometimes bad things happened to nice folks. After all, she was a textbook case.

"I'm sorry for you both." She meant it. However, be that as it may, she still had to get out of here. She was in enough trouble without being dragged into the middle of Johnny and his fiancée's mismatch.

"You know," he continued, holding up a hand and urging her to wait, "I should have realized this last year. Before we formally announced our engagement. But I grew up with Felicity. Her family and mine have done business together since before either of us was born. We played army in the hay mow together. Her mother changed my diaper upon occasion. I knocked out several of her baby teeth when I convinced her to let me back flip off the high diving board with her in my arms when we were seven. She hit the board on the way down."

Emmaline winced.

"The point is, all my life, everyone has just assumed we'd marry. Even me. It never really dawned on me to question that. Until now. Until I saw the guest list. And the presents. And the honeymoon itinerary." He passed a hand across his eyes, over his jaw and around to the back of his neck in a gesture that spoke of his tension.

"Suddenly it all came so clear in my mind. We weren't little kids anymore, playing together out in the sandbox. We are adults who, through no fault of our own, are just not right for each other. And, we never will be. Ever."

"Mmm." Emmaline exhaled in sympathy. He was in a jam.

Muscles twitched in his jawline, and Johnny stared unseeing out the window. "I'm going to call the wedding off. In the long run, it wouldn't be fair to anyone to go through with it. No matter what, I can't subject Felicity to a loveless marriage. I may not be in love with her, but she's been a good friend all my life, and I like and respect her. It's better that Felicity and I call it quits now than after we've been married and she's begun to set up housekeeping."

"That's...uh—" Emmaline cleared her throat "—true enough." She nodded in agreement, although she was still puzzled as to why he'd run from one loveless marriage straight into another. Especially with her, of all people. Surely she had far less to offer than Felicity and her connected family. And, as she adjusted her glasses higher on her nose and studied the tiny frown lines on his handsome face, Emmaline knew that her own physical attributes weren't the calling card here. "But why marry me?"

"Because the Lowenstone family and our family are about to become permanently entrenched in the megamerger of the century. Felicity's dad, of the Lowenstone Oil Corporation, and my dad, of Brubaker Industries are on the verge of buying out Magtron Oil. If they do decide to go into business together, I don't want it to be because Felicity and I marry. I want it to be because that's what they want to do. A divorce between Felicity and me could cause untold friction between our families. I need to call off the wedding before they sign the papers."

"Mmm." Logic was something Emmaline could relate to.

Johnny refocused on her. "That's why it suddenly dawned on me that we could kill several birds with one stone, with a business-deal-type marriage. Felicity will be devastated as it is, but this way, she won't have to feel quite so…uh…personally rejected."

"No, she'll simply feel cheated on." Emmaline watched as emotions warred behind his beautiful cobalt-blue eyes.

"She already does," he muttered, propping his elbows on his knees and plunging both hands into his hair. Lifting his head, he peered up at her through bleary eyes. "She heard your rather vehement declaration when you arrived."

"Oh, dear." Emmaline groaned. "I'm so sorry."

"You couldn't have known." He drew a deep breath then slowly let it out as he leaned back against the plushly upholstered couch and stared at the ceiling.

"Would you like me to go explain about my mistake to your family? To clear things up?"

Lolling his head on the pillowy headrest, his gaze traveled back to her. "No. That's the point I've been trying to get across. You see, with you in the picture there won't be any going back for any of us. Felicity will be forced to get on with her life, whether she wants to or not. And our fathers will have a chance to duke it out before they sign on the dotted line." A rueful grin tipped his lips as he continued.

"After all these years, I know this much about Felicity. If I just tell her that I don't want to get married, she'll hold out hope of changing my mind. She is as persistent as a hungry she-bear and twice as tenacious. This way, as painful as it may be for her right now, it will force her to move on. To get on with her life. And, as far as being unwilling to say die goes, my dad and hers are even worse than she is. Big Daddy Brubaker and Gus Lowenstone never take no for an answer. Unless—" Johnny's glance darted to Emmaline's midsection "—there is an issue of family at stake. Then Big Daddy can be made to see reason. Family is everything to him."

Emmaline placed a protective hand over the little life, deep in her womb. "Family?"

His gaze followed the path of her hand. "Giving the baby a name would be part of the deal, yes. As far as anyone but you and I need know, the child will be a Brubaker."

She slung her purse strap over her shoulder and once again Emmaline mentally prepared to leave. She had to get out of here. His offer was becoming more attractive by the minute. Giving the baby a name—a good, well-respected name—in the community was very appealing, considering her rather dire circumstances. Plus, a wedding, hasty or otherwise would certainly smooth the path with her family and the people who funded her research grant. And the fact that it would only last a short time was compelling, as well.

Emmaline had no burning desire to marry for love now or in the near future. No. Her passion lay in finding out exactly how genes and cancer cells work at the molecular level. A business deal with Johnny Brubaker made more sense than it did not.

Still, the very idea was ludicrous. Her gaze traveled over his strikingly handsome face and across his rugged, rangy build. Who would ever believe a love match between the two of them? She had to talk some sense into him, before his life was sucked into the sewer alongside her own.

"Isn't marriage, even as a business agreement, a little rash? Good heavens, Mr. Brubaker—"

"Considering that I have just proposed marriage, it would probably be okay if you called me Johnny." His family's classic, signature dimples leaped out of hiding to bracket his sexy mouth.

Emmaline couldn't help but stare. He was far better looking than the guy at the wedding, and that was saying something. Crazy as a loon, but cute in a well-meaning but misguided kind of way. "Okay, er... Johnny, don't you think you are jumping out of the marriage frying pan and into the fire?"

"Not if we're going into this thing knowing that it will be a business deal from the beginning."

Hmm. Business was not her forte. Most likely he knew best in that realm.

Johnny leaned forward and looked her full in the eye. "Since we will remain emotionally uninvolved, I can't see how either of us can be hurt once it's over. As part of the agreement, I'll make sure the baby's scholastic future is secure—"

Suddenly, Emmaline's heart screeched to a stop and began to churn in reverse. The baby's scholastic future? Good heavens. A wave of panic washed over her at these words. Of course. Her child would have to go to college. That was a given. All Arthurs went to college and obtained a fistful of degrees and a doctorate or two along the way.

It was family tradition.

This was yet another thing she hadn't had time to contemplate since finding out that she was pregnant. How on earth was she going to send Junior to college on her sporadic income? Grants came and grants went. Today she could be flush, tomorrow scrambling.

She made good money, for a single gal with no expenses. But raising a child? She wasn't equipped! She couldn't do this. What was she thinking, trying to do this on her own?

And what would she say to the poor kid when he or she finally got around to asking about Daddy?

Her ears rang and buzzed in her head. She was trapped. By her own idiocy. She guzzled her second glass of sparkling water, then pressed the cool crystal to her forehead. Hands shaking violently, she knew she was losing it. She had to focus. Biting down hard on her lower lip, she tried to concentrate on what Johnny was saying.

"—and another trust fund when he or she is eighteen. So you would have no worries in that regard. And in the meantime, it will give us the perfect refuge within which to hide out, and…you know, regroup. You can continue your—" a slight frown marred his brow "—what is it you do?"

"Cancer research. I work at SystaMed Labs with Nora."

His brows rose in appreciation. "Wonderful. Great. You can continue your research, and I'll continue to run the ranch here at Circle BO. We'd lead separate lives, except when we are called to do something social as a married couple. It will be important for us to maintain that facade at the very least… " His voice trailed off as the wheels in his head spun.

"I...no...we can't..." Emmaline sputtered, groping for what was left of her sanity. Try as she might to come up with some reason that would refute his bizarre logic, she couldn't. As much as she hated to admit it, he was making perfect sense.

They didn't love each other. Never would. It would be strictly business. She could continue her exciting research without a hitch. He needed her. She needed him.

The baby needed them.

"Deal?" He extended his hand to seal the pact, his face boyish and vulnerable in its expectation.

Closing her eyes, Emmaline felt as if she were jumping off an ocean liner without a lifeboat. For a moment she tried to envision her future if she refused his generous offer, and couldn't. On her own there was no happily-ever-after scenario for herself. Which didn't really matter in the scheme of things. But she was no longer alone in this world. She had a child to think about now. A child whose reputation and financial and educational future mattered. At least to her.

Tentatively she held out her hand only to find it enveloped once again by the powerful, labor-roughened grip that inspired such an amazing sense of security in her. She shook her head. How had accepting a simple wedding invitation from Nora led to her own wedding a mere month later? It was insane. No matter. She was here and she would make the best of it.

"Deal."

# Chapter Four

Five afternoons later found Johnny in his one-bedroom suite in his parents' mansion. The suite he would soon share with Emmaline. And eventually, the baby. He was preparing for his wedding, just as he had known he would be doing on this very day for the past year. The only difference being that today, the bride was not Felicity Lowenstone.

As Johnny leaned toward the antique cheval mirror and fastened his collar studs, he could still hear the echo of Felicity's histrionics reverberating in his head. To say that she had not taken the news of his supposed infidelity well, was an understatement.

After Felicity had stormed off in a Porsche-red streak, tires squealing, dust flying, he'd introduced his rather shell-shocked parents to Emmaline. They had been very gracious to Emmaline, all things considered, hiding their emotions to the best of their ability until they were in private. They had even been a little—

though they would never admit it at the moment—happy about the baby.

It seemed that no matter how a youngster arrived into the Brubaker fold, it would be received with open arms by his loving parents. Knowing their moral code, the fact that Emmaline came to them pregnant and was so unconditionally accepted, only increased Johnny's sense of guilt and betrayal. However, he had to keep telling himself that what he was doing was for the best. For everyone concerned. In his shoes, he wondered if his father might not do the same.

He and Emmaline had agreed not to tell his parents the truth about the baby's father until after they'd taken their vows.

As he reached for his tie, Johnny allowed his gaze to stray out the window and into the rose garden two stories below. White wooden folding chairs had been set up on the smaller of the three brick patios and an aisleway, strewn with rose petals, had been fashioned down the center. A white tent, festooned with flowers and candelabra, was positioned down front to afford the best view of the bride and groom as they exchanged their vows. The giant laurel hedge and various topiaries had been strung with tiny white lights that sparkled in the afternoon's twilight shadows. In the background, the stringed quartet began to tune their instruments, and the soothing burble of the various fountains played a natural accompaniment.

Johnny liked this paired-down version of the ceremony much better than the extravaganza that was to have taken place. Right now, the very last of the preparations were being made for the small, rather informal family gathering. The minister had arrived and Big

Daddy was making somewhat forced, yet jovial, conversation with Emmaline's parents.

Moving closer to the window, Johnny peered down at the scene below as he tied his bow tie and straightened his starched collar. Emmaline's parents were standing in a patch of sunshine, seeming decidedly out of their element. As he stared at the frumpish Mr. and Mrs. Arthur, Johnny could see where his bride had learned her dowdy sense of style. Both parents sported the same bottle-bottom glasses that Emmaline favored, and they had obviously used the same machete blade to trim their own tresses. In a fashion that had them looking more like twins than husband and wife, they parted their dull brown hair down the middle and combed it flat to the skull. They were both wearing brown suits, practical shoes and carrying large leather bags that looked to be stuffed with books.

As he wrapped and fastened his cummerbund around his waist, Johnny could also see where Emmaline had developed her love of academia. Last evening, when he had first made the acquaintance of his future in-laws, they had seemed distinctly disappointed that he only had a bachelor of science degree from a state university under his belt.

Ah, well, he mused, turning away from the scene below to shrug into his tux jacket, they would be rid of him soon enough. Per his and Emmaline's legal agreement, they would be divorcing three months after the birth of the baby. Then she would be free to pursue the Poindexter of her choice.

And Johnny would at last be free to get on with his own life. To find a woman that suited him and his lifestyle. A woman of strength. Of substance. Of gentle humor and a quick wit. Someone bright, but not uptight, someone practical, spontaneous and, if he was lucky, loving. And, if he was very lucky, someone attractive, both inside and out. Oh, not a raving beauty. Stunning good looks had never been all that important to Johnny. However, someone softer than Felicity and with more fashion savvy than Emmaline would be nice. A set of great legs wouldn't hurt anything, either, he thought with a wry smile as he buttoned his jacket. But that was for the future. He had plenty of time to find his soul mate. After he'd had a chance to enjoy his bachelorhood.

With one last inspection of his reflection, Johnny decided he'd pass and left his suite to join his brothers in the library for the traditional glass of brandy, cigar and brotherly pep talk on the dos and don'ts of a happy marriage. Too bad they were wasting their breath. Although, he had to admit, a cigar and a glass of brandy would not be lost on him at this juncture.

With only a little more than two hours left to go, Emmaline couldn't be sure if the nausea she was feeling was from her pregnancy or from the terror she felt at the thought of walking down the aisle and committing a year of her life—and that of her unborn child's—to a man she'd only known for a week. A man who was not even the father of her baby. Seated at the vanity in the immense bathroom of one of the suites that Miss Clarise had designated as the bridal preparation area, Emmaline reached over and turned on the cold water and allowed it to cascade over her wrists.

What was she thinking?

That had been the first question her parents had

asked upon their arrival out here at the Circle BO, last night.

"But why?" Mr. Arthur had wanted to know over dinner the previous night. "Why the big rush? Why not enjoy a long engagement and have the wedding next June?"

Her mother had looked equally perplexed. "What about your research? That's your whole life, Emmaline. Certainly you will want to continue working."

Fortunately, between Emmaline's bewildered expression—which her parents had taken as lovestruck—and Johnny's glib charm, they had accepted the news without too much fuss. Slipping his arm around her shoulders, Johnny had flashed his dimples at her parents and smoothly explained.

"Emmaline and I are going into this marriage with our eyes wide-open. Both of us feel that waiting until next year to tie the knot would be a waste of precious time. Time that we could be spending together, getting started on little Johnny junior. Of course, Emmaline will continue working until we have a baby. After that, we'll play it by ear."

With that, he'd cast his soulful gaze into Emmaline's, stealing her breath and rendering her speechless. Too flustered to protest any further, Emmaline's parents had simply nodded.

And now, she thought, staring at her reflection in the bathroom's wall of mirrors, here she was, mere moments from taking her sweet father by the arm and literally leading him down the garden path. Emmaline sighed. Why did life have to be so complex?

Her father was a proud man. He hadn't taken the news that Johnny would be funding the wedding well at all. However, when he'd insisted upon buying the happy couple two nights at a fancy hotel in Dallas as a wedding gift, neither Johnny nor Emmaline could say no. Tears gathered on her lower lashes as she thought of her darling father's tender expression as he'd handed over the sentimental card and the enclosed check. Oh, how she detested lying to them this way.

Her parents didn't know about the baby. Both she and Johnny felt it would be best to make that announcement to the rest of the family next month, after their supposed minihoneymoon. Emmaline exhaled from deep within her lungs as she dried her wrists on the embroidered hand towel.

"Here she is! Back here in the bathroom. Perfect!"

Patsy Brubaker Lassiter, Johnny's only sister, burst—along with her entourage of both family, friends and strangers—through the suite's double doors, her face beaming with excitement. Forced from her worrisome ruminations, Emmaline turned her attention to her future sister-in-law and the unusual-looking man she dragged along behind her.

"Hi, Emmaline." Patsy was breathless with excitement over her brother's impending nuptials.

Patsy had been studying dance in Europe when her three older brothers had tied the knot, so this was her first opportunity to really involve herself in the festivities. And, involve herself she did. With gusto. Emmaline could fairly hear the engine's whistle as she was cheerfully railroaded through her wedding day.

"Emmaline, you remember Holly? Buck's wife?" Patsy offhandedly gestured to her sister-in-law who was carrying a box heaped with corsages and bouquets. "And your friend Nora is around here somewhere. Oh, there she is, behind Mama." Nora waved, and Miss Clarise, her arms loaded with gowns, peeked over the organza, casting a gentle smile in Emmaline's direction. "And we have someone to do your nails and makeup and this—" she declared in triumph as she tugged the hand of her mystery man "—is Max, from Maxim's Impressionistic Hair, Los Angeles. We had him flown in, just for you! What do you think, Max? We only have a couple hours…"

Rolling his eyes, Max sashayed forward and grabbed a handful of Emmaline's dull locks.

"Egad, woman," he screeched, his diamond-encrusted fingers flashing as they dove into her tresses, pulling and yanking, inspecting and massaging. "I hope you have a good lawyer, because whoever did this to your hair should be shot!"

Emmaline winced. "Uh, I…I did this to my hair."

Max caught her eyes in the mirror and raised a droll brow. "Then you, my dear, should be shot." Pursing his lips, the harried hairdresser swirled his fingers through her lifeless hair, clucking and tsking and grimacing as if he were in great pain. Finally he threw his hands up in resignation. "Oh, well, never mind. No use crying over bad hair. Max is here to save the day." Yanking off Emmaline's glasses, he tossed them to Patsy. "Good grief, honey, those things must weigh six pounds. How can you stand it? They do nothing for your looks. I'm sure you must have some looks in there somewhere. We simply need to find them and bring them out."

Good luck, Emmaline thought and shrugged.

To Patsy he commanded, "Throw those hideous specs away, sweetie." With a self-satisfied smile, he turned back to his victim. "You go get you some new glasses some other day, girlfriend."

"But…" Emmaline sputtered and blinked, trying to focus. "I need those glasses today. I can't see very well without them."

Grabbing Emmaline's chin, Max tilted her head back so that he could peer into her face. "Can you see me?"

Eyes wide, she gazed up at him. "Uh…yes."

"It's your wedding day and honeymoon, sweetie. This—" he blew air kisses at the tip of her nose "—is all you need to see." Releasing her chin, he snatched up his scissors and set to work.

With a resigned sigh, she leaned back and let Max wrestle with her wayward hair, even though it seemed like a colossal waste of time and money. No use trying to make a butterfly out of a moth's wings, she mused. It wasn't as if she tried to have such horrible hair. It was simply a matter of genetics. Max need only to look at her parents to see the light.

Nope, she was a plain Jane, no bones about it. And she'd done a pretty good job of convincing herself that she liked it that way. She had been blessed with intellect. With such a gift, who had time for the added social burden of beauty? That was such a transitory thing to begin with. Today's beauty queen was tomorrow's plump granny, so why stress? Fads and fashions were just so much useless energy spent.

Besides, what did it matter if Johnny found her beautiful or not? This was a business deal, pure and simple.

Oh, well. She would humor his family today. Actually, it was kind of cute the way they were so eager to help, wanting to do something nice for her on her big day. And, she had to admit, being pampered this way made her feel just a bit decadent.

The hours flew by and suddenly everyone left and Emmaline was alone.

Max had done what he could with her and then gone back to Hollywood where he belonged. All of Johnny's female family members and her friend Nora had dressed in a whirlwind of activity. They'd donned corsages, applied last-minute makeup and chattered like excited magpies the whole time. Emmaline would have loved to have shared in their enthusiasm. But this was a business deal. No use getting carried away with some fantasy.

Johnny stood, his legs spread slightly for balance, his hands clasped tightly behind his back, and watched his three-year-old niece, Crystal Gayle Lassiter, come skipping down the aisle. The audience was comprised of her cousins, her uncles, grandparents and a smattering of Emmaline's friends from SystaMed, some of the science students she tutored and the church choir.

Flexing his shoulders, Johnny attempted to distract himself by looking out over the various faces. The Lowenstones, having angrily bailed out of the megamerger to acquire Magtron Oil, were conspicuously absent; although, no one had expected them to attend. Felicity's temper had been obviously inherited from her father, Gus Lowenstone. On the bright side, Gus had already found another partner, and the merger was targeted to take place only slightly behind schedule.

For a moment Johnny considered calling off this business deal with Emmaline, but decided it was too late now. His brother Kenny and his cousins Dakota and Montana were standing up with him, black-and-white barriers to freedom in their tuxes. That was all right. As far as business propositions went, this one would require relatively little effort. He simply needed to live with Emmaline for a year. Linking his fingers behind his back, he cracked his knuckles.

The string quartet created an ethereal backdrop for his three sisters-in-law as they step-paused, step-paused their way one at a time down the aisle. He rotated his shoulders to ease the tension, and his gaze shifted to his sister, Patsy, as she moved toward him, a beatific smile on her face. Relishing her role as matron of honor, Patsy had taken Emmaline under her wing much the way a swan would mentor an ugly duckling.

Johnny had fully expected that Emmaline would have wanted one of her own friends, such as Nora, to act as matron of honor at her wedding, even though this was not a conventional marriage. However, it was becoming increasingly apparent that his bride had never taken enough time from her studies or her work to forge close relationships of any kind. And though she was involved with several community activities, she was for the most part a loner. Johnny liked that about her. After Felicity's constant social tornado, it was blessed relief.

Patsy winked at him as she moved past and took her place with the bridesmaids. His heart picked up speed. The arrival of the matron of honor up front always signaled the entrance of the bride.

The pace of the classical music slowed, paused, then resumed as the wedding march. Amid much rustling and neck straining, the hundred or so guests all stood and turned to catch a glimpse of the bride. Mr. Arthur had changed clothes since Johnny had last seen him standing beneath his window. Much to his surprise, Emmaline's father looked nearly dapper in his rented tux. The old man's ruddy complexion was flushed even ruddier with pride as he reached into the rose trellis and withdrew his daughter, tucking her hand into the crook of his arm.

Fleeting thoughts passed through Johnny's mind. The fact that Emmaline was an only child suddenly struck him. Giving his daughter away had to be rough on Mr. Arthur. If he was ever lucky enough to have a little girl of his own, Johnny knew giving her away to some young cowboy wasn't something he'd relish. Too bad he couldn't reassure the old man that he was only borrowing his daughter for a short time.

A gauzy veil floated about Emmaline's face obscuring her expression as she clung to her father's arm and began her slow ascent up the aisle. The guests were all beaming and for an exhilarating moment, Johnny could almost imagine that this was for real. That the woman moving toward him in a cloud of satin and lace was his true love. The woman of his dreams.

His eyes glazed over.

From where he stood, she looked lovely. The dress clung to her freshly pregnant curves, boosting some impressive cleavage above the dainty seeded pearl neckline. Her skin was smooth and creamy in the twilight, and her hands, delicate and sporting polished longer nails, rested on the black fabric of her father's jacket.

If Johnny didn't know better, he'd swear that Emmaline had chickened out and sent a stunt double to stand in for her. A graceful stunt double with touchable-looking shoulders.

After what seemed to Johnny to be an interminable amount of time, Emmaline and her father finally reached the altar. The music came to a poignant crescendo, then died.

The minister, Pastor Dodge, the very same man that had married, christened and baptized most everyone in the Brubaker clan for as long as Johnny could remember, stepped forward. "Who gives this woman in marriage?"

Mr. Arthur's voice, shaking with pride and emotion turned and announced, "Her mother and I do." He kissed his only daughter through the netting of her veil and handed her reluctantly off to Johnny.

As she grasped her fiancé's hand in a grip that would have had a less-prepared man wincing, Emmaline moved to stand next to Johnny at the altar.

"Dearly beloved," the minister began, a contented smile on his face as he addressed the crowd, "we are gathered here today to join this man—" he looked Johnny directly in the eyes, then shifted his gaze to Emmaline where it settled with warmth "—and this woman in holy matrimony. A marriage," he boomed, hitting his stride, "is a sacred covenant between two people..."

Johnny stilled, his brows drawing together at the solemn words. Holy matrimony? Sacred covenant? Is that what this was?

In his zeal to bail everyone out of a difficult situation, he'd forgotten the truest meaning of the wedding vows. As the minister's voice droned on, Johnny stole a sideways peek at Emmaline. It was hard to tell what she was thinking beneath all that gauzy netting but, if the death grip she had on his hand was any indication, she was sweating bullets over this part, too.

Setting his meaty fists on Johnny's and Emmaline's shoulders, the portly minister turned them with a gentle touch to face each other. "The wedding ring is a symbol of the love and respect that these two people feel for each other. It is a public declaration of their love...."

Johnny peered at the veil that covered Emmaline's face and wished to hell that he could see through it to her eyes. He hadn't counted on the emotional impact of this ceremony. Shifting his gaze over Emmaline's shoulder, he could see his sister, already misting up, and beyond Patsy his parents were looking on, the pride and tears evident in their faces, as well.

Ah, shoot.

He felt lousy, faking them all out like this. But, it couldn't be helped. A lot of people's future happiness depended on this ceremony. As the solemn words of sanctity were recited, Johnny phased out and thought of the other times he'd heard these vows exchanged. In his family these were forever words. Words that bound. Words that united. Words that turned two into one. One unit. One spirit. One...flesh. In fact, right now he could almost feel Emmaline's hand melding with his.

Before he knew what hit him, the minister was calling for rings and they were getting ready to promise to love, honor and obey until death parted them. Death. Hopefully this charade wouldn't kill him.

"Do you, Johnny Cash Brubaker, take Emmaline to be your lawfully wedded wife?"

The words had become a jumbled mishmash in his brain, reverberating, echoing, searing like a hot knife. Until death parted them. For worse. In sickness. Death, death, death. Again he strained to see Emmaline through the opaque fabric that covered her eyes, to no avail.

"I do," he heard himself answer. Fumbling on autopilot, he slid the simple band of gold onto Emmaline's finger to rest alongside the brilliant diamond solitaire they'd purchased only the day before.

"And," Pastor Dodge continued, turning to face Emmaline, "do you, Emmaline Marie Arthur, take—"

Again the words of doom taunted him. Until death. Death, death, death.

"I do," Emmaline murmured, her voice quaking. Hands trembling, she pushed the matching ring over Johnny's knuckles and onto his finger.

He flexed his left hand. It felt strange.

As Pastor Dodge pontificated on about the sacred holiness of this wonderful thing that he and Emmaline had undertaken to do, Johnny felt as if a spike of remorse had been driven through his heart. This would have been a whole lot easier, had they simply run down to the justice of the peace. The muscles in his jaw worked to the point that his teeth began to ache. However, he knew he had disappointed his folks so much already over his broken engagement to Felicity. Going through this ceremony for them and Emmaline's parents was the least he could do.

Pastor Dodge beamed at them. "Insomuch as you have both promised, in front of these witnesses—" he indicated the audience with a sweeping gesture "—to stand by each other until the end of your lives, by the power vested in me by the great state of Texas, I now pronounce you husband and wife." Broad belly bouncing beneath his ceremonial robes, Pastor Dodge chuckled. "Folks, I'm proud to introduce to you, for the very first time, Mr. and Mrs. Johnny Brubaker. You, sir," he said, clapping Johnny on the back, "may kiss your bride."

Johnny stared at him for half a beat before he realized he was supposed to give Emmaline a kiss. Right. Of course. He needed to kiss the bride. Everyone did that at weddings. He wrestled with the masses of netting, until he found his wife's face.

And he froze.

Confusion gripped him as he stared at her, taking in this new version of the Emmaline he thought he knew. Holy matrimony! She was...she was...good heavens almighty, she was beautiful! In rapid-fire succession, his fuzzy mental faculties tried to rationalize this woman with the woman who'd just promised to be his business partner for the next twelve months.

Her hair, once mousy and limp—the way he liked it—now framed her face in a feathery haze that had somehow become gossamer with light streaks of gold. It looked eminently chic and soft as an angel's wings. He hated it! Her eyes, luminous and unfettered by her cumbersome glasses were now fringed by dark lashes and lids artistically smudged with a pearlescent taupe shadow. High cheekbones were drawn out of hiding by an artist's brush and her lips, a soft plumb, begged his kiss.

Dammit. What had Patsy done to her?

He wasn't supposed to feel this kind of attraction toward Emmaline. This desire that suddenly blindsided him was wrong. It didn't matter that she was now his wife. This was a business deal. Nothing more.

Johnny flexed his hands in the tangle of netting as this microcosm of suspended time allowed him to study his bride. She was not the same woman at all. This was not good. Uncertainty gripped him by the throat. He wanted his old business partner back. The frumpy, dowdy, uncomplicated Emmaline Arthur, brainiac researcher, with whom he'd found an acceptable level of comfort. The woman who did nothing for him sexually speaking.

The minister cleared his throat.

Someone in the audience twittered.

Emmaline's eyes flashed back and forth into his, searching, wondering, looking distinctly rattled herself.

Unfortunately they'd never discussed the odd time when they would need to perform public displays of affection. Most business arrangements were not sealed with a kiss. They hadn't discussed protocol for such an event. Over Emmaline's shoulder, Johnny could see the worried looks on the faces in the audience. Everyone was holding their breath, himself included.

Unable to stand the tension another minute, Big Daddy blurted out, "Well, son, are y'all gonna kiss her, or stare all dopey-eyed at her all night?"

"Hush, Big Daddy," Miss Clarise chided.

"Well, *I* don't recall having to be told twice," the old man grumbled.

A rumble of laughter rippled across the crowd.

Cocking his head, Johnny lifted and dropped his shoulder, wondering how to best approach this situation. Taking a step toward Emmaline, he figured he couldn't very well not kiss her. It was obvious everyone was expecting him to do something. Okay. He would keep it chaste. A token peck of affection. No big deal. They would laugh about it later.

Slowly he released the netting he'd been clenching in his fists and allowed his hands to travel to her face, where he cupped her delicate cheeks. Her minty breath fanned his lips as she sighed and closed her eyes, her darkened lashes resting on porcelain skin. Suddenly

Johnny felt himself turned on, in a way he'd never thought humanly possible. In a way that transcended the physical. That transcended all logic. All rational thought.

Oh, this was definitely not good for business.

Angling her mouth beneath his own, he hesitated for a split second before settling his lips upon hers and at that moment he could have sworn that his heart ceased to beat. Her lips were warm and soft and pliant and open for his kiss.

All thoughts of chastity flew out the window.

He didn't know—when it came to kissing Emmaline Marie Arthur-Brubaker—exactly what he'd expected, but it sure as heck wasn't this. She arched toward him, and he instinctively took another step into the folds of her voluminous dress, drawing her more firmly into his embrace. Her arms stole up over his shoulders, and her fingers found home in the hair at the nape of his neck as naturally as if they'd been kissing this way forever.

His own hands slid from her cheeks into the silky cloud of her hair, and though he knew he should pull away he instead hauled her up against his chest and deepened the kiss.

And she responded.

Oh, baby, how she responded. Lightning flashed behind his eyes, planets collided, atoms split. Johnny knew in the back of his mind that the kiss had gone on far longer than was appropriate—even for a couple deeply in love—but he couldn't seem to stop himself. Never had he ever felt anything like this with Felicity. Or any other woman, for that matter.

Surely, Emmaline must be able to feel the stampede of wild horses that was his heartbeat galloping against her breast. A tiny whimper escaped her throat, and Johnny had to tear his mouth from hers before he embarrassed himself in front of his entire family by attempting to consummate their business arrangement right there on the spot.

Somewhere in the background someone whooped, and everyone giggled.

Chest heaving, he staggered back a step and stared at her, in shock.

"One more time," someone else called, and again a wave of laughter rippled into the evening air.

No. No, he couldn't.

It wasn't supposed to be like this. It was supposed to be platonic. Not plutonium. He struggled for self-control, already angry that he'd allowed her that moment under his skin. They had a deal. He needed to stick to it, or risk losing it all together.

"Go on!" someone called and the crowd began to clap.

Having no choice, and worrying that folks might think it odd if he refused, Johnny stared grimly at Emmaline. Okay. One more time. But this time he'd keep his throbbing libido under control. This time he would feel nothing. Per their agreement.

Groaning, he pulled his new wife roughly back into his embrace for another kiss. Oh, man, it was going to be a hell of a long year.

# *Chapter Five*

Still in shock from not only the first kiss, but the subsequent kisses that had left her head in a mindless muddle, Emmaline walked down the aisle on the arm of her new husband and wondered what kind of brazen hussy she was becoming.

Good heavens. She had practically thrown herself at Johnny during that third kiss, her cleavage heaving against the pleats of his shirt, her breathing ragged, her heart failing. And then, when it would have been proper—nay decent—to gracefully pull away, she'd strained toward him once again, melding their mouths, tugging at the back of his head, urging him on in such a wanton manner that surely he'd only complied to save her from disgracing herself in front of God and everyone. Like the true gentleman that he was, he'd suffered her enthusiasm until the laughter in the audience had become so deafening that he'd ripped his mouth from hers and set her at arm's length.

His face had been flushed a brilliant shade of crimson and he'd looked positively thunderstruck. It was obvious that she'd embarrassed him beyond words. She berated herself in silence for her uncharacteristic rash of stupidity. Honestly, she didn't know what had come over her. Ronny had made it perfectly clear that she had no talent whatsoever in that regard. What did she think she was doing?

However, during that first kiss, when his lips, so soft and warm, had covered hers and then with a subtle pressure nudged them apart, her brain, usually so dependable, so analytical, so…so…discerning, had failed her for the second time in her adult life. Once again she'd thrown caution to the wind and decided to let herself enjoy this new experience. Her first real experience kissing a real man.

Ronny hadn't been much on kissing. She cringed at the thought of Ronny's energetic pawings. He'd gotten right down to business, skipping the romance of which Emmaline had always dreamed.

And now Emmaline was sure that allowing herself this bit of reckless abandon with Johnny would find its way back to haunt her as well. He would no doubt be filing for divorce before the week ended.

If she was lucky, maybe she could persuade him that it had been temporary insanity. Stage fright. And then, to prove her point, she would simply steer clear of him. She was no clinging vine.

"This way," her new husband muttered, guiding her up a short flight of brick stairs. His mood seemed to have darkened considerably since he'd become a married man. It was all her fault. She'd trespassed upon the no-sex clause of their agreement, and they hadn't even made it across the threshold of their suite at the hotel.

"Thank you." Emmaline loosened her grip on his arm.

"You all right?"

"Fine."

"Sure?"

"Yes," she snapped. He needn't spend the day leading her around and worrying, especially when it was obvious how disgusted he was. Well. She was perfectly capable of taking care of herself. She tried to pull away but only succeeded in stumbling over a loose brick.

"Careful." It was a command.

Yes, keeping her distance from Johnny Brubaker in her emotionally vulnerable state was an excellent idea. She vowed to put the kisses from her mind and never think of them again. Ever.

Blinking back the tears of mortification that threatened, Emmaline knew she couldn't afford to louse everything up with some kind of adolescent crush now. She had her baby's future to consider. From where she stood, she could make out the low murmur of her parents' voices. They sounded so proud.

"Right over here." Johnny's words were politically correct, but his delivery was grimly in check.

Emmaline bit the inside of her cheek to keep from crying. Had she already burned the bridge? His chiseled lips, forming a grim line, were the only things in focus in her otherwise completely blurry world. "Thanks."

"No problem."

By now the sun was balanced at the edge of the western horizon, casting long, gentle shadows in this second, more secluded courtyard. A warm, balmy Texas breeze flirted with Emmaline's veil and voluminous skirts and the heady scent of roses filled the area.

As Emmaline stood with Johnny, receiving endless congratulations from the multitude that made up his family and assorted close friends, she became increasingly melancholy and found herself wishing that she were truly a part of this clan and not simply an outsider looking in. How on earth she would endure twelve solid months of fooling this lovely family was beyond even her superior ability to fathom.

The string quartet had been moved to a raised platform that sported a grand piano, just off to the side of the patio's largest fountain. Several more musicians had joined the group, turning it into a small orchestra that was now warming up with a festive waltz.

Grabbing a microphone, Big Daddy leaped up to the podium at the side of the bandstand, and cleared his throat.

"Evenin' everybody!" Beaming with joy, he waited until he had captured the crowd's attention. "As soon as Emmaline and Johnny, here, have greeted y'all, they will lead off by sharin' the first dance together."

Emmaline felt Johnny stiffen at her side and didn't have to look at him to know that this was the last thing he felt like doing.

"After that," Big Daddy continued, "a big ol' buffet table, loaded with every kind of delicacy will be spread out over yonder in the third brick patio. Y'all can enjoy a sit-down, candlelight dinner. Then—" a gleeful light entered his eye "—there will be some speech makin' and toastin' and we'll have Emmaline chop up that good-lookin' cake."

Shortly after Big Daddy's enthusiastic speech, the folks at the end of the line arrived, paid their respects and the orchestra began to play a waltz for the sole enjoyment of the bride and groom.

"Shall we dance?" Johnny plowed a hand through his hair.

Eyes cast to the floor, Emmaline shrugged. "It's expected, I suppose."

"Yes, it's expected."

She sighed, knowing the last thing she should be doing at this point was dancing with Johnny. Her options vanished as he held out his hand and she followed his rigid lead to the center of the patio. Though she couldn't see much beyond arm's length, Emmaline knew that everyone must be watching, much the way that Nora's friends had watched Nora and her husband dance at their wedding last month. Had it only been a little over a month ago? Seemed like a lifetime.

As he took her in his arms, Johnny's expression went blank, and he began to sway to the light strains of the waltz.

After she'd gotten the hang of the simple steps he was leading her through, Emmaline touched her tongue to her parched lips and decided that now would be as good a time as any to set the record straight.

"I'm sorry about the kiss. I mean, I didn't know…I didn't expect…" She struggled to find the words that would make him understand that he had nothing to fear from her. That she could be trusted.

His eyes darted from hers to some point off in the distance. "No, no. I'm the one who should be sorry." He blew out a heavy breath. "I should have known that was coming."

Emmaline stumbled. Was she that transparent? That needy? "Oh?" The tops of her ears grew hot. Having no choice, she clutched his arm and righted herself, climbing over his booted toes in the process. Luckily, he didn't flinch.

"Unfortunately, I'm afraid that before the day is through, we might have to…perform—" his eyes flashed back to hers "—again."

Emmaline couldn't sustain his gaze. "Perform…again?" She hated the way her voice sounded so high and breathy. What did he mean, *perform?* She didn't think she could survive another kiss.

Johnny regarded her for a moment, unnerving her. "You don't have to look so afraid. I promise we'll keep it to a dull roar this time."

Humiliated, Emmaline nodded dumbly. "Of course, I can do that. Don't worry about me. I'll…I'll… that's…that's what we originally agreed to. That's what we should stick to, by all means. I—" she swallowed "—I'm just sorry we have to put on this show."

"Can't be helped. They have expectations." He lifted and dropped a shoulder. "I guess if we are going to convince everyone that this is a real marriage and not just some words on paper, then we will have to behave like newlyweds now and then when people are watching."

"In public only. I understand." His message was coming through loud and clear. Emmaline nodded, and he seemed to relax some.

The music swelled and increased in tempo. As Johnny swept her around the dance floor, Emmaline felt so light she couldn't be sure that her toes were actually touching the bricks. She struggled to shove the ebullient feelings the dance evoked back into some dark, unused corner of her heart. But it was hard. Never before had she worn such a dress and danced with such an amazing man. For a moment, Emmaline felt almost...carefree. Luckily for her Johnny's lead was so effortless that even a stumbling neophyte such as herself appeared expert at the art of the waltz.

His now-familiar scent of herbal soap and expensive cologne—mixed with the vaguest hint of cigar smoke and brandy—teased her nose. His body was rock hard beneath her fingertips and at the same time, warm and comfortable. Too comfortable. Pushing a little more space between their bodies, she chanced a glance at his face. His sexy mouth was looming, mere inches from her own slack lips. She pushed a little harder.

Brows arched, Johnny glanced down at the space between their bodies. "Since everyone is watching, we should probably be holding each other a little tighter, for now."

"Tighter?" she croaked.

He peered into her face. "Less loosely?"

"Do you think that's wise?"

A puzzled frown marred his brow. "Wise?"

"For us to...uh...touch so much?"

In his jaw a tiny muscle throbbed. "It's all right. For now."

Though her head bobbed in understanding, she'd never been so confused in her life.

"Your parents seem to be enjoying themselves."

"They do? I can't see them."

Johnny inclined his head. "They are over by the punch bowl. Smiling at us."

"Smiling?" Emmaline strained to see in the dwindling light, but it was hopeless. "That's rare. Usually this kind of affair is not within their comfort zone. We—" She debated for a moment how much time she should waste telling him about herself, considering their union was headed for ultimate dissolution. On the other hand, a little conversation might relieve some of the tension. "We never had company when I was a kid. My folks were always too busy tending to my education or their careers." Feeling wistful, she looked up at him. "You were lucky, growing up in a household full of parties and celebration."

Johnny snorted. "I'd prefer to hang with your folks, I think. I'm a homebody at heart."

"There must be a happy balance in there somewhere."

"I'm sure. Smile, my folks are watching."

"Mmm." Her lips stretched up at the corners.

"So are yours."

"That's nice."

"In fact, everyone is watching."

Emmaline would have to take his word for that.

He cleared his throat. "This number is coming to an end. I think it's time for a little public display of affection."

"Time?" Emmaline's stomach roiled uncomfortably. Exactly what did he have in mind now?

"It's expected."

"Of course."

The music came to a soft end, and the watching crowd began to clap. Johnny reached for her hands and, bringing them to his lips, kissed them one at a time. "That should be enough to get us by," he murmured.

Emmaline stared at him, her hands shaking and clammy as she clutched his for balance.

Still up at the podium, Big Daddy snorted into the microphone, the porcine sounds reverberating from speaker to speaker. "Kiss your bride properlike, boy," came his gleeful urging.

"Yee-haw!" One of the ranch hands shrieked, and again, the crowd broke into spontaneous applause.

Only Emmaline was privy to the ice in Johnny's eyes as he flashed a glacial glance up at his father.

"Sorry about this," he muttered, pulling her into his arms before either of them could change their minds. The orchestra struck up another sweeping dance number, and as they swayed to the music, he lowered his head, and his lips sought hers. And—just as she'd feared during the first kiss—Emmaline could swear that her heart was about to plunge through her cleavage. Once again, she trod on his toe, but he didn't seem to notice.

His lips settled over hers, probing, teasing, driving an incredible ache into the pit of her stomach. Deliberately she kept her eyes open, fighting the sensations and concentrated on the waltz. One-two-three. One-two-three, she chanted in her brain as he murmured the sweet nothings of the typical enamored groom against her mouth, then planted tiny kisses along her jaw before settling his lips and tongue against the side of her neck.

Someone moaned and she had the sneaking suspicion it was herself. One-two-three. Her eyes slid closed and her spine was on fire. The flesh on her arms and shoulders was icy with gooseflesh. If it wasn't for the tap on Johnny's back, Emmaline would surely have had to have been carried off the dance floor on a stretcher.

"I said kiss her, son. Not ravage her." Big Daddy's laughter was infectious, and everyone within hearing distance was smiling.

Nearly dropping Emmaline, Johnny stared at his father through dull eyes. "What do you want, Big Daddy?"

"May I have a turn around the dance floor with your little gal?" Big Daddy boomed, his shuffling feet itching to sweep his newest daughter-in-law a time or two around the dance floor.

None too pleased by the intrusion, Johnny cleared his throat and took a step back and handed her off to his father.

Johnny stood looking after them, feeling edgy and disgruntled. It seemed that no matter how hard he tried, he couldn't kiss Emmaline and feel nothing. At this point, he doubted that even her ugly glasses and drab summer suits would cool his ardor.

"Well?" Patsy's bubbly tones reached him from behind. "What do you think? Doesn't she look good?" Slipping her hand through the crook of his elbow, she tugged her reluctant brother to the dance floor and forced him to waltz with her.

"Too good," he grumbled. For the entire number he was unable to tear his eyes from his bride. Jaw dropping, he watched over his shoulder as his handsome cousin Dakota cut in on Big Daddy. Emmaline smiled demurely and, obviously flustered, danced more on his toes than the bricks.

Muscles at the back of Johnny's neck clenched so he rolled his head to ease the knots.

Patsy studied her brother's face, then threw back her head and laughed.

"What's so funny?" he demanded.

"You're jealous."

"I am not."

"Are, too." Again Patsy hooted. "Oh, now, baby

brother, don't go getting all bent out of shape just because your cousins have suddenly noticed how lovely your bride really is.''

Together they watched as Montana tapped his brother on the shoulder and nudged him out of the way. Luckily Emmaline couldn't see well enough to notice how Dakota limped off the dance floor. Even so, he still looked pretty beguiled by the awkward bride. There was something about Emmaline's sweet, social innocence that Johnny had to admit was downright compelling.

Patsy cupped Johnny's cheek with the palm of her hand and urged him to look into her eyes. ''You know, she only has eyes for you.''

Johnny stilled. That was not good. But nevertheless, he took a certain amount of pride and relief in her words. He could feel Patsy's probing gaze and knew she most likely sensed that something didn't exactly add up between his new bride and himself. Forcing himself to exude a nonchalance that he didn't feel, he smiled at his sister.

''Having fun?'' he asked.

''Mmm. You?''

''Yep.''

''Bet you can't wait to get out of here and get started on your honeymoon.''

Johnny stumbled. ''I...we...''

''A little nervous?'' Again Patsy threw back her head and laughed. ''That's just how I felt on my own wedding night,'' she confided. ''And it was wonderful.''

All too soon the reception was over and the honeymoon had begun. For lack of something better to do in the honeymoon suite she now shared with her new husband, Emmaline decided to unpack.

After the reception, she'd rescued her glasses from the trash. She put them on now, to better see in the low light. Emmaline sucked in her breath as she bent over her suitcase and fumbled through the mishmash that lay in her suitcase. Stunned, she held up one bizarre thing and another, frantically trying to locate her chaste flannel pajamas. But it was hopeless. Beads of sweat dotted her forehead as she vacillated between fainting and just plain passing away.

Patsy!

Who else could it be? Johnny's mischievous sister had ransacked her suitcase, taking out her T-shirts and pj's, her comfortable cotton panties and her sensible bras and replaced them all with a pile of the most scandalous looking underwear she'd ever seen. Her entire body caught fire with mortification. Holding up a skimpy lace thong—whose most important parts were missing—to the light where she could better inspect it, she could no longer contain her shock and gasped.

"Lord, have mercy!"

"What's wrong?" Johnny asked, from where he sat in the corner, perusing the wine list.

"N...nothing."

She whipped around to face him, pushing the panties and the matching scrap of a bra behind her back. Certainly this would not cover anything! Johnny would think she'd gone around the bend for sure if she wore this stuff.

Emmaline glanced down at her attire and her shoulders slumped. Unfortunately, thanks to Patsy, the only thing she had left to wear for the rest of their weekend together, was her wedding dress. She supposed she could dig up a pair of manicure clippers and saw off the hoop skirts, the ridiculously long train and the whale-bone stays, but this dress had belonged to the women in Miss Clarise's family for generations. No doubt her new mother-in-law would not see the beauty in the improvements.

She was going to kill Patsy once she found some clothes.

Dropping the menu, Johnny stood and moved toward the bed where Emmaline's suitcase lay, a tangled mass of feathered and sequined lingerie strewn over the bedspread. She scrambled to rake it all back into a pile.

"Unpacking?" His voice was droll as he came up to stand behind her. Picking up a neon-pink garter belt he allowed it to dangle over his fingertips.

Emmaline cringed. She could feel his eyes practically boring a hole through the back of her head. No doubt he was wondering just what kind of nut job she was. Breathless with humiliation, she attempted to explain.

"I...no...you see, I thought... I was looking for my regular—" Feeling hopeless, she sagged and held the peekaboo bra with the strategic heart cutouts up for his inspection. "Your sister."

"Ah."

His tone indicated that she needed no further explanation, and for that Emmaline was exceedingly grateful.

"I, uh, I don't have anything to wear. Except—" she clutched the lingerie to her chest "—this stuff. And, of course," she amended, gesturing at the ungainly mass of satin, hoops and frothy netting that comprised her voluminous wedding dress, "this."

"Can't wear that all weekend." There was more than a hint of amusement in his voice.

She shook her head. "At least not to bed." Visions of hoops straining vertically under the covers flitted through her mind. No bride, even a pregnant bride marrying only for convenience, wanted to bring an image of pup tents to her groom's mind on her wedding night. She battled an hysterical urge to cry. It had been a long, emotional day, and she wanted nothing more than to simply sleep.

"Hang on. I'm sure I have something you can wear to bed."

He hoisted his own suitcase up to the bed alongside hers, and rummaged for a few moments, a perplexed frown suddenly furrowing between his brows.

"What's wrong?" Emmaline ventured, sensing by his body rigid body language that all was not well.

"Patsy."

"Uh-oh." Emmaline peered into his case as he pulled out the few meager items of clothing that were left. Together they found one pair of boxer shorts emblazoned with indecent suggestions about the care and handling of the owner, several pairs of multicolored bikini-type briefs for men, a pair of Hefner-type silk pajamas and a bag of toiletries.

Emmaline felt a rush of heat travel up her neck and settle in her cheeks.

Looking down at his own wedding garb, Johnny blew a thoughtful breath out of his mouth. "Well, I'd offer you my shirt, but it's nothing but a false front of pleats and a collar." He shrugged out of his tux jacket and tossed it on the bed to better display. "See? It's custom-made. The cuffs attach to the jacket sleeves. My tailor swears it makes the lines smoother, or some such cock and bull. As you can see, the vest isn't much better.''

Emmaline could see the smooth flesh on his back and arms and knew that there was no way that either of them could wear that silly thing for the next two days. The vest was comprised of a false front and two elastic bands across the back that held it into place. Fascinated, she watched as Johnny—looking like one of those Chippendale dancers she'd seen once on cable TV—stripped off both pieces and held them up for her inspection.

"So, I guess you'll have to share my pajamas. Why don't you take the top and I'll take the bottoms.''

"I…uh…guess that makes more sense than you taking the top and me—'' she pulled her lower lip between her teeth ''—taking the bottoms.'' Her mouth had suddenly gone dry. He was magnificent.

"Sure.''

She held up the man's silky pajama top Patsy had included. It wasn't much, but it was better than nothing. "Well, I suppose I should go…get dressed.'' Hoping her bright smile belied her myriad qualms, Emmaline began to back toward the bathroom door.

Her wedding dress lay in a mountainous heap across the marble ledge of the whirlpool tub built for two. Feeling cold and unbelievably foolish in the skimpy pajama top, Emmaline leaned over the sink and peered into the mirror. She looked absolutely ridiculous.

She shrugged.

Whatever. Weary to the bone, she was beyond caring. After she'd brushed her hair till it shone and her teeth till they sparkled, she picked up a bunch of cotton balls, soaked them in some cleanser and began scrubbing her face.

Staring at her reflection she wondered who this woman was staring back at her. This woman who had married one of Texas's most eligible bachelors only hours ago. This woman whose first baby was due sometime come spring. Surely this woman could not be herself. She tossed the used cotton balls in the garbage and blinked at the changes Max had wrought.

She certainly didn't look the same anymore. Twisting her wedding set on her finger, her thoughts strayed to Johnny. Nor did she feel the same. Though, she guessed both changes were probably an improvement over the drab persona she'd hidden behind for so many years.

Before he'd gone home to L.A., Max had given her a barrage of instructions on skin care and a whole bag of makeup, facial cleansing and hair care products as a wedding gift and insisted that she make a habit of using them. Grumbling and fumbling through this disgustingly expensive bag of tricks, Emmaline tried to remember what it was that Max had said she was supposed to put on before bed. Gracious, her memory wasn't what it used to be. Hormones. Had to be.

Lifting and dropping her shoulders, she turned on the faucet and proceeded to scrub her face with a good old-fashioned washcloth and a bar of soap, the way she'd done all her life. Most likely, Max would be hyperventilating if he could see her now, but that was his problem. She had enough on her mind.

After drying her face on a fluffy white bath towel, she rummaged through the bag and found some lovely smelling lotion which eased the tight feeling on her cheeks the soap had caused. Just for fun, she slathered some on her hands and legs as well. Umm. Felt like silk. Probably cost just as much, too.

Dreading going out into the bedroom to face Johnny in the far too short pajama top, she sat down at the vanity and continued to play with the cosmetics Max had given her. She'd never owned a cosmetic bag, filled with expensive goodies of her own. It had simply never seemed necessary. Not that it seemed necessary now.

She was stalling.

Stalling and hoping that Johnny would be asleep by the time she emerged from the bathroom. Would he think it odd if she slept in the tub?

She'd like to blame her curious emotions, her heightened awareness of her appearance and her feelings of sexual awakening on the fact that her hormones were running wild because of pregnancy. But she couldn't. Emmaline knew, deep within her heart, that the answer lay with the man in the next room.

The man wearing nothing but pajama bottoms.

Oh, mercy. It was going to be a long, blankety-blank year.

After what seemed like eons to Johnny, his bride scurried out of the bathroom. She looked nervous.

Even as his heart went out to her, it skipped a beat or two at the sight of her lithe, yet sturdy body. Again he was taken aback by secrets revealed, which she'd managed to so successfully disguise with her bulky clothing till now.

As she flitted across the room like a butterfly looking for a place to light, he was completely discouraged to discover that she had beautiful legs.

Criminy. His sigh was tinged with agony. He was a leg man. Nothing he liked better than a graceful, shapely pair of gams that seemed to go on forever. Aw, hell. As much as he didn't want to notice, he simply couldn't tear his eyes away from Emmaline's delicate ankles and perfectly sculpted calves.

Man, oh man, her legs were the stuff his fantasies were made of. The last thing he'd needed to discover tonight was her legs. He stifled a groan and attempted to bring his suddenly elevated pulse under control with some deep breathing.

"I'll, uh, I'll just…" Emmaline stammered as she cowered behind the bed and dragged her suitcase in front of her scantily clad body to shield his view, "I'll just, uh…put these things away…"

"You can have the closet." He made this offer knowing that he certainly wouldn't be needing it for a couple pairs of shorts.

"Okay. Good. Thanks." Holding the suitcase across her midsection, she backed awkwardly into the closet, where she disappeared behind a mirrored sliding door.

As one minute passed into another, Johnny's smile of amusement faded. What the devil was she doing in there? Finally, after a quarter of an hour ticked by, he was unable to stand the suspense. Pushing himself off the couch where he'd been watching baseball on ESPN, he ambled over to the closet and slid the door open.

"Emmaline?"

"Yes?" Her muffled response came from the other side of the sliding door. She was sitting on the suitcase holder using as a handkerchief one of the lacy scraps his sister had provided, dabbing at tears that pooled in the corners of her eyes.

"You gonna stay in here all night?"

"No, no. Of course not." Her smile was tremulous as she peeked out from under the hangers that dangled just above her head. "I was, uh, just looking for one of those terry cloth robes that these nicer hotels are supposed to provide. I've looked and looked," she babbled on, her voice cracking with emotion, "but I can't seem to find one."

"Oh. Well, don't cry, honey, maybe that's not one of the amenities this chain provides. I bet if we looked, we could find a shower cap around here somewhere." He teased her, hoping to make her smile. She looked completely miserable.

"Well, I want a robe." She sniffed. "My father probably spent a bundle on this room. We should at least have a stupid robe."

Johnny leaned against the closet's doorjamb and glanced at his watch. "I'd offer to send out for some stuff for us to wear, but it's after midnight. I doubt that we'd have much luck finding anything open at this hour."

"Of course. You're right. It's okay, really."

She hiccuped and dabbed some more at her eyes, and Johnny had to fight the unhealthy urge to join her in the closet and take her into his arms. Playing it cool with a woman in distress had never been one of his strengths.

Especially one who was such a wreck. How could he, in good conscience, ignore her? Johnny reluctantly decided that he could resume his cold-shoulder act once they were both properly dressed and she was feeling less vulnerable.

"Listen, it's late and in your condition, you need rest. Why don't we call it a day and go to bed."

She blanched. "I…um…we…"

Understanding her angst, Johnny smiled. "You take the bed. I'll take the floor. If you don't mind parting with a blanket and a pillow."

"Oh, you shouldn't have to sleep on the floor. That hardly seems fair."

Might not be fair, but it was the only way he'd be able to keep his sanity over the next year. They couldn't sleep together and certainly he couldn't expect a pregnant woman to sleep on the floor.

Brightening some, she blinked up at him. "Maybe we should call housekeeping and order a rollaway bed."

Johnny grinned. "This is the honeymoon suite, Emmaline. Personally, I don't want word out around town that my bride and I slept in separate beds on our wedding night. We're a pretty-well-known family in these parts. Word gets around. Felicity would have a field day with that bit of gossip."

He watched as an endearing crimson flush crawled up Emmaline's face and settled in her cheeks. Damnation, she was cute, sitting there half-dressed, blushing like a schoolgirl.

"Oh." She cast a dubious peek over at the bed. "Well then, I guess I'll take you up on your offer. If you're sure."

"I don't mind. Honest. I'll be happy as a clam. We have to sleep on the ground whenever we drive cattle. I'm used to it."

"Well, okay." Her smile was grateful. Stifling a yawn, she awkwardly maneuvered her way out of the closet and then dashed pell-mell to the bed where she ripped back the bedding, dove under the covers and pulled them up under her chin.

Johnny followed her to the end of the king-size bed and pulled his suitcase onto the padded bench. Once he'd snagged his toiletries bag, he gestured toward the bathroom.

"I'll just go get ready for bed now. If you want to toss out a pillow and a blanket, I'll sleep over here on the floor."

"Okay."

"I'll only be a second."

"Okay. Uh, Johnny?"

"Yeah?"

"Could you turn off the air conditioner? Without my regular pajamas, I'm kind of cold."

"Sure thing. I'll turn on the heat and warm it up in here for a few minutes."

"Thanks."

"No problem."

Emmaline watched as he moved from the thermostat to the bathroom and shut the door. While he was gone she wrestled the bedspread off the bed. As she tugged the ungainly spread from between the footboard and the mattress, her thoughts swirled and her emotions whirled. A wave of homesickness for her familiar little bed in her familiar little apartment washed over her. Swallowing against the lump in her throat, Emmaline tossed the heavy spread onto the floor beside the bed and threw a pillow on top of that.

She flopped back against her own pillows and tossed her glasses on the nightstand.

The door handle to the bathroom rattled, and Emmaline pulled her covers up under her chin and, for want of something better to do with her malfunctioning gaze, shut her eyes.

\* \* \*

Johnny emerged from the bathroom and glanced over at Emmaline. She looked to be asleep. That was quick. Well, good. The less contact he had with her, the better. He moved quietly around the room and snapped off all the lights. Then he found the pile of bedding she'd left for him and, fumbling in the darkness, made himself as comfortable as possible.

He'd lied about loving to sleep on the ground. These days when he went out to drive cattle, he took the motor home. Complete with king-size bed. He'd have to figure out something better than this, in his and Emmaline's room, back at the ranch. Sleeping on the floor for a solid year was out of the question.

Finally, after much blanket arrangement and pillow punching, Johnny found a reasonably comfortable position and began to relax. Although, he feared visions of a leggy woman in a silky pajama top would no doubt keep him awake for hours.

"Johnny?" The whispered word floated through the darkness, a lilting melody, teasing his libido.

"I thought you were asleep."

"Not yet. Are you…are you comfortable down there?"

"Yep."

"Okay. I can spare another blanket, if you want."

"I'm fine. But thanks."

As his eyes adjusted to the darkness, he could see Emmaline outlined in the moonlight that filtered in through the crack in the blackout curtains. Leaning on her elbow, she'd propped her head up on her hand. One ankle was thrust out of the covers, leaving a shapely foot dangling over the edge of the mattress. How was he going to last for an entire year with those legs within arm's reach of his lousy bed on the floor?

Giving his pillow a vicious punch, he attempted to put it out of his mind. He'd think of something.

"Can't sleep?" she asked.

"No," he grunted. "You?"

"Uh-uh. I guess I'm too keyed-up from all the wedding excitement." Her sigh was breathy.

Johnny flipped onto his back and stared at the ceiling. "Yeah. Me, too."

"Oh." She inhaled deeply then expelled her regrets about the wedding, like so much bad air. "Again, I want to tell you how sorry I am that we had to go through all of this rigmarole, just for a simple business deal. I—" she paused, and he could almost hear her wince "—didn't mean for it to get so…personal."

Johnny dragged his hands through his hair. She was no doubt referring to the way he'd mauled her at the wedding and reception. Somehow he had to convince her that she didn't have to worry about that happening again. Now that the wedding was over, they could much more easily lead separate lives.

"Don't worry about it."

His tone was a little more forceful than he'd intended, but he was worried. That kiss had changed everything. Feeling bad in the shadow of the silence that ensued, he softened his voice. After all, it wasn't her fault that he couldn't keep his hands to himself.

"Hey. It's all over now. Let's just forget it, okay?"

"Okay."

There was a melancholy note in her tiny voice that made him want to smooth things over. "It wasn't a total loss of a day," he offered, looking for something benevolent to say. "Everyone had a good time, I think."

"They seemed to."

"My family likes you."

Emmaline was quiet for a moment as she digested this bit of information. "Why? I would think after what they believe I did to Felicity, they would hate me."

Johnny's chuckle was rueful. "I don't know. I think they will all be grateful to you in the future."

"Oh." She didn't sound too sure about that, but seemed willing to give him the benefit of the doubt. "I like your family, too. They're nice. So different from mine."

"Yeah. They're a good bunch. I want to kill Patsy most of the time, but the rest of 'em are keepers."

Emmaline laughed and then grew thoughtful. "You sure have a lot of cousins. How do you keep them all straight?"

Johnny could hear her plumping her pillow, settling in and getting ready for a conversation. Since neither of them would be sleeping for a while now, he figured they might as well kill some time by chatting about his family. It would help keep his mind off the kisses they'd shared that afternoon. The kisses he couldn't seem to force from his mind.

"Well, it's not too hard keeping 'em all straight, if you just remember that my father's younger brother, Tiny Brubaker—"

Emmaline's lilting laughter made him smile. "Tiny? Your family has the strangest names. He must be even smaller than your dad, if Big Daddy is the 'big' one."

"Nope. Big Daddy is only the big brother because he is a year older. Actually, Tiny's a giant bear of a man. Makes Big Daddy look like a leprechaun."

"No! Really?" There was a smile in her voice.

"You know, the odds of that happening within the same gene pool are really very slim."

"Luckily, you're right. All of us boys—Tiny's and Big Daddy's—ended up at around six foot one or two."

"From your description, I gather Tiny wasn't at the wedding? I think I'd have remembered dancing on his feet."

"Right. He and his wife, Bernice, had to go to a funeral on Bernice's side of the family this weekend. But, I'm sure you'll get a chance to meet him before we—"

There was a stilted silence.

"Anyway," Johnny continued, feeling that it was in poor taste to discuss their divorce on their wedding night, "he and my dad are best friends and at the same time, archrivals."

"Typical for male siblings, close in age."

"Yeah, but these guys are extreme. They are so competitive that whenever one of 'em had a kid, the other one would get mad and have two more. When Tiny had four boys and Big Daddy had three, Patsy was born and she was the light of Big Daddy's life. So Tiny went on to have five girls just to spite him, my dad says."

Emmaline hooted. "That's impossible."

"Tell it to my dad. Anyway, they kept building their broods until they each had nine and our mothers forced 'em to call a truce."

"I should hope so!" She giggled, shuffling around under the covers to find a new, more comfortable position. When she'd done that, her voice was tentative as she asked, "You don't want that many children do you?"

Johnny guffawed. "Are you kidding?" He stretched his arms up over his head. "No, I have no desire to compete in the great Brubaker baby competition. One or two—three at the very most—is more than enough."

"I think you're wise. Nobody should have to go through morning sickness for nine years of their lives."

"That bad, huh?"

"Not if you like the interior view of a toilet."

They laughed together.

"No, I don't want to have nine kids," Johnny confessed. "Unless I follow my brother Buck and my sister Patsy's lead and adopt a passel of kids that don't have anyone or anything."

"Oh, I think that sounds lovely. I always wanted my folks to adopt some brothers and sisters for me, but they were so busy with their studies that they just never, I don't know…" Emmaline burrowed into her pillow. "So, tell me," she murmured sleepily. "Did Tiny name any of his kids after country-western singers?"

"No, he went in another direction. Tiny is probably the most patriotic man you'll ever want to meet. That's why he named each of his kids after states in this 'great country of ours.'"

"Which would explain Dakota and Montana." The bed shook with her giddy, overly tired-from-pregnancy-and-marriage laughter. "That's a riot. So there are nine states altogether?"

"Mmm-hmm."

"Okay, wait. Don't tell me their names. Let me guess. Let's see, there must be a Mississippi and a Rhode Island in there somewhere," she giggled and rolled onto her stomach to better hang out over the edge of the bed, "and...um..." she sounded as if she were growing slightly punch-drunk.

No wonder. The red LED numerals on the clock boasted the small hours of the morning. It was a miracle she was still awake after such a big day. Johnny's smile widened.

"...um...a set of twins, oh, yeah, East and West Virginia...and then...of course we can't forget the triplets, New Mexico, New Jersey and uh...New... New Hampshire!" Laughing, she let her arms flop over the edge of the mattress, her fingers accidentally tangling in his hair. "Oops, sorry about that." She patted his head and withdrew her hand.

"You know, I like that." He was referring to more than just the name but decided not to go there. "I think we should consider New Hampshire for our own bundle of joy. We could call him or her little Hammy."

"Yeecch." Emmaline giggled.

Her laughter was infectious, and soon he found himself laughing as hard as she was. There was something about being dog-dead tired and lying on the floor that increased the hilarity.

"Ohh, Hammy," he called, sing-song, "come in for dinner."

"Sounds like Hammy is the main course."

They guffawed and howled and made rude Hammy jokes until they were both gasping for air. And it was then that Johnny realized that he'd probably had more fun with Emmaline in this silly conversation than he would have had with Felicity on their entire round-the-world honeymoon cruise. Funny how that was.

"I'm serious now." Johnny sighed in contentment.

"I think Hammy Brubaker is the perfect name. No one else will have it."

"Oh, please. No way."

"Even if there is a country-western singer named Hammy?" He pretended to pout.

"Nope. Not even if there is a Hammy Wynette somewhere out there. With my looks—" she protested, hanging over the bed "—and that name, the poor kid will never flourish."

"There's nothing wrong with the way you look."

Emmaline snorted, but made no comment.

Deciding to take a different tack before he blurted out something he'd regret later, Johnny moved back to the subject of the names Tiny had chosen for his children.

"Anyway, sadly you are wrong about the names of my cousins—with the lone exception of Virginia—on the states Tiny chose for his own little darlings."

"Oh, boo. I hate to be wrong."

"Well, get used to it. You're part of a big family now. Everyone is wrong at least twice a day."

"Not me."

He could tell she was teasing. "Okay, for you, three times a day, because you're new."

"Ha."

"Anyway, let me finish here, will you?"

"Go on," she said, yawing broadly.

"Am I boring you?"

"Yes, but in a good way. It might help me sleep."

He snorted. "I aim to please. Anyhow, there are four boys, Dakota, Montana—those two yahoos were at the wedding today. They stood up with me and danced with you—"

"Yes," Emmaline murmured good-naturedly. "I know the tops of their boots intimately."

"I noticed."

"Was I that bad?"

"No, just the belle of the ball. As it should be, for the bride."

"Well, I'm sure I didn't make much of an impression."

"I wouldn't count on that." He ran his hand over his jaw. Emmaline had danced with all of his cousins, brothers and friends today, and for some odd reason he'd been so uncomfortable with the idea, he'd gone back to claim her for himself, not letting anyone else cut in for the rest of the evening. She commented that it was because he was rescuing the toes of his male kin. But unfortunately that hadn't been the reason at all. He'd wanted to dance with her. To have her make mincemeat of *his* toes, dammit.

"You may remember," he continued, forcing his mind back to safer ground, "that you met the rest of 'em in the receiving line. There was Tex and Kentucky who goes by Tucker."

"Yes, I recall. I like those names." Emmaline stifled another yawn. "Almost as much as I like the singer names."

"They're hard to forget, that's for sure."

"What did he name the girls?"

"Well, there are five girls. You were right about Virginia, who everyone calls Ginny. Then there is Carolina, Georgia, Maryland, who goes by Mary and last but not least little Louise-Anna. She's still in high school."

"Where—" another yawn "—do they live?" Emmaline asked, her voice sexy with drowsiness.

"They have a huge spread, not too far from the Circle BO, but Tiny has more oil fields than we do on his ranch. Most of our oil fields are off campus, so to speak. So, we have more ranch land. That's why Tiny is renting a couple of our sections to run his cattle. Dakota and Montana have been working on our ranch for about a year now, giving me a hand. They'll probably quit and go into their daddy's oil business eventually. But until then, we're all having a little fun running the ranch until Tucker and Tex and my brother Kenny take over for us."

"Sounds…like—" there was a long, sleepy pause "—fun."

"It is. I can show you around the back sections later this week, if you're interested."

Slow, even breathing was her only response.

Johnny tucked her foot back under the covers and wished that he could nod off so easily.

Later that night Johnny woke up in a pool of sweat. He'd been dreaming of Emmaline. They were trapped in a sauna together, and she was naked except for some wild, beaded and feathered underwear. Her legs were not, he was chagrined to find, the only shapely thing about his wife. And she'd kissed him again and again, pulling him toward her, sending him into orbit. But no. He had to resist. He had to fight. They had a legal agreement. Someday, someday, someday, he would find a real wife. One who met all of his specific requirements. Until then, he had to cool off.

He gave his head a firm shake to clear it of the cobwebs.

Aw, man, what a nightmare.

Tossing back the covers, Johnny stumbled to a standing position, using the edge of the bed to right himself. Damn, it was hot in here. Must have forgotten to turn off the heat before he hit the hay. Doing that in June in Texas was a dumb mistake.

Staggering to the thermostat, he flipped it to AC then moved to open a fogged and sweating window. Surely it had to be cooler outside than it was in. He cranked open the small glass pane and a whoosh of crisp predawn air caressed his feverish skin. Nudging back the heavy black-out draperies, he opened several more of the little windows and inhaled the fresh air.

Ah, that was much better.

He turned and cocked a hip against the wide window ledge, crossed his arms over his chest and studied Emmaline as she lay on the bed. She'd shucked all of her covers, and his pajama top had ridden up around her waist. In the early-morning twilight, he could see that her skin was damp with a sheen of perspiration. In repose, she was an angel, her face relaxed, her usual pensive, thought-heavy expression eased into sweet innocence. He longed to crawl in next to her and press his body against that silky top she was filling out so nicely.

Someday, he mused, pushing off the window casing, she'd make some lucky guy a hell of a decent wife.

For now he was going to hit the shower. A long cool blast of water was just what the doctor ordered.

"Johnny!"

At the sound of Emmaline's voice, Johnny shut off the faucet and peered in surprise through the mottled glass at the frantic face of his wife. Her eyes were practically bugging with urgency.

"Johnny," she hissed, "hurry!"

Cracking the shower door, he poked his head out and grinned. Had to be something pressing to get her to come in here and roust him out this way. Must be the call of nature. He knew from his sister and sisters-in-law that when first pregnant, they were in and out of the facility with a regularity that rivaled the precision of Big Ben.

"Hand me a towel," he gestured to the fluffy stack, "and I'll clear out and leave you alone."

"No!"

He frowned, puzzled. "No?"

"Someone is out in the hall, knocking on our door. You're not going to believe this, but I think it's our parents!"

# Chapter Six

Emmaline stood behind Johnny as he peered through the peephole in their door. Water dripped from his hair to his shoulders then sluiced in little rivulets down his torso and into a towel he wore wrapped loosely at his hips. Shivering, more from embarrassment than from lack of warmth, she ran her hands over her legs to discourage the gooseflesh.

"Well?"

Holding his finger to his lips, he turned and nodded at Emmaline. "Yep, it's them all right."

"All of them?" she whispered, aghast. Brow wrinkled, her jaw dropped in disbelief.

"All four of them."

"You're kidding."

"I wish." Jerking a thumb behind him, he said, "Run and pick up that blanket and pillow that are on the floor, then hop in bed." He began to disengage the various locks that adorned the door. "I'll be over there with you in a second. Just try to remember, we are newlyweds and act accordingly, okay?''

"Okay.'' She was too flustered to worry much about the whats or hows of the typical newlywed behavior as she flung the bedspread into the already-mangled pile of covers.

Johnny had barely cracked the door to their suite when the beaming Big Daddy came barreling through.

"Mornin', you two lovebirds.''

Following with obvious reluctance, Miss Clarise and Mr. and Mrs. Arthur, stepped into the room, all flushing crimson with mortification. Johnny hiked his towel a little higher at his hips and stared at his father.

Oblivious to the discomfort of everyone in the room but himself, Big Daddy bestowed a wide grin upon his new daughter-in-law. "Mornin', honey pie!''

Smile weak, Emmaline nodded and tucked her covers up under her armpits. "Morning.''

"Big Daddy—'' Johnny shot a glance over at Emmaline "—it's not even 7:00 a.m. yet. What on earth are you doing here?''

And, when will you leave? Emmaline wondered, but was far too polite to ask.

Big Daddy chortled. "Since your folks holed up with us last night and we offered to take 'em to the airport this mornin' for their bidness meetin' in up there Chicago. And, being that your hotel just happened to be right on the way, well, I wanted Emmaline and her folks to have a chance to say their goodbyes.'' He doffed his hat at the three he'd dragged along for this impromptu gathering. "They didn't know we were coming here.''

Mr. and Mrs. Arthur nodded. "We didn't know.'' They cast an apologetic glance at Johnny.

"It's true." Miss Clarise agreed. "We're as surprised as you two." There was a murderous twinkle in her gaze as she eyeballed her husband.

Rubbing his hands together, Big Daddy fairly vibrated with glee. "Are you surprised?"

"To put it mildly." Johnny's expression was droll. "Good!"

Johnny drove his hands through his still-wet hair. "How did you find our room?"

Big Daddy's boisterous laughter rang out causing the genteel and proper Miss Clarise to roll her eyes and sigh. "You'd be surprised what you can get for a couple of C-notes around here."

Johnny wore the pained expression of an impatient lover, and Emmaline had to admit, he was a pretty credible actor. If she hadn't known better, she'd be tempted to think that he was truly eager to be alone with her.

"You know, Big Daddy," Johnny cast a dour look at all four parents, "we were planning on a leisurely morning in bed before we start our day. Right, hon?"

"Uh..." Emmaline sat fossilized with stupefaction.

Johnny perched on the edge of the mattress next to her, and draped a casual arm around her shoulders. He stared pointedly at his father. "Sorry about our skimpy attire, but we weren't really expecting company."

"Not that we mind, of course." Emmaline's smile was bright. Come to think of it, perhaps there was safety in numbers. With their family near by, she didn't have to worry about spending the day in such close proximity with her sexy new husband.

"I do," he muttered through clenched teeth. Bringing his lips to her ear, he whispered for her sole benefit. "We're supposed to be on our honeymoon. Start acting like it. If we were really in love, we'd want them out of here.'' He planted several kisses at Emmaline's temple. ''Just go along with me. If we make 'em uncomfortable, they'll leave and we can relax.''

Having no choice, Emmaline simply nodded as Johnny nuzzled her neck and played up his role as ardent young bridegroom. Goose bumps flared like wildfire from the flash point of his lips and down her arms and legs. Under other circumstances, in a different time and place with a different husband, she might have been tempted to enjoy the attention. As it was, she sat, simply frozen, trying to arrange her face into the euphoric picture of wedded bliss.

As Big Daddy rustled up some chairs so they could settle in for a visit, Mrs. Arthur clutched her husband by the arm and inched toward the door. They stood side by side, looking completely nonplussed—two beet-red, brown-tweed, lumpy, frumpy birds of a feather. Their eyes darted everywhere but at their scantily clad daughter and her amorous, bare-chested husband. Emmaline's heart went out to them. It was obvious that they were absolutely mortified.

She knew the feeling well.

Johnny grabbed her hands and placed them on the nicely sculpted muscles that formed his broad chest. ''Keep me warm, darlin'. I don't want to get a chest cold,'' he cajoled, an endearing pout teasing his lips. Holding her wrists, he moved her floppy hands in energetic circles around the gentle swell of his pectorals.

''Would you knock it off?'' she hissed under her breath, smiling broadly at her mother as Johnny rotated her arms hither and yon across his body.

''Newlyweds,'' he hissed back, also smiling Cheshire-cat fashion at his in-laws. ''Remember, we're newlyweds.'' Still gripping her wrists, he continued to maneuver her less-than-willing hands over his torso, occasionally bringing them to his lips for some little palm kisses.

Emmaline could only shrug and smile half-heartedly at her parents as her hands became acquainted with her husband's sinewy body. She struggled to don a mask of normalcy—nay, joie de vivre—for her parents' sake.

Unable to stand another awkward moment, Emmaline's parents opened the door. ''We really hate to run, but we always like to get to the airport early. Important conference. Have to go. It's been planned for ages. Right, dear?''

Mrs. Arthur nodded, still at a complete loss for words.

''Well, thank you for stopping by...Mom...Dad,'' Johnny said with a cordial bow of his head.

''We'll just show ourselves out. Emmaline, we will call you when we get settled in at the conference hotel.'' Both Mr. Arthur and his wife took a step toward their daughter, as if to kiss her goodbye, but had second thoughts and merely waved instead.

''We also must run.'' Miss Clarise lifted a meaningful brow at her husband.

''But we just got here.''

''Big Daddy,'' her tone brooking no argument, Miss Clarise fired her words like the bullets from a gun. ''We must run. The Arthurs need a ride to the airport.''

When their parents were finally gone, both Johnny and Emmaline flopped back against their pillows and sighed.

"I think we did a pretty credible job of convincing them all that we're mad for each other, don't you?" Johnny arched a questioning brow at his wife.

"Ohh, yeah." There was a sardonic quality to her voice that had him grinning. "I don't think any of them could have missed the way you had me mauling your body."

Johnny's hearty laughter shook the bed. "I have to admit, that was a stroke of genius."

Emmaline's sigh was dramatic. "Whatever. I'm just afraid my poor parents may never recover from the shock."

"Oh, get over it. They know the score. They must have made love at least once in their lives. After all, you are here."

"True. However, I'm sure they waited until they had no audience before performing the…uh…the deed."

Again, Johnny howled with laughter. "Oh, now, I don't think I did anything all that scandalous. Considering," he teased, gesturing to the towel he wore at his hips, "I could have really given them a show. Like this, for instance." Snorting and growling, he rolled her beneath his body and kissed her neck until she was helpless with laughter. "Umm. You smell good."

She knew it must be the fragrant lotion that Max had given her, as Johnny inhaled a path along her neck to her shoulders and arms, planting little kisses as he went.

"Let me up, you big…you big…blankety-blank boob."

"Oh." Johnny feigned a wound to the heart. "She's cussin' now."

Emmaline's shoulders bobbed with laughter. "Will

you get off me?'' She squealed, pushing at his chest as he hovered over her. ''Our parents are gone. The show is over. You can stop now.''

''And, what if I don't?'' Suddenly he was less playful and more intent in his ministrations.

''If you don't, then I'll…I'll…''

''Ye-e-s?'' He cupped her face between his hands and brought her mouth beneath his for a kiss that rivaled in its intensity, and perhaps surpassed, the one they shared at the wedding.

''I'll—'' she gasped, losing herself in the moment ''—I'll try…try…I'll try to remind you, sir…of our…of our…agreement.''

As her words penetrated his passion-fogged mind, Johnny suddenly became acutely aware of his state of undress, and the fact that he was dabbling with something that could easily sabotage a perfect business deal. She was right. He'd allowed himself to become swept away in the moment. Something he couldn't allow to happen again.

Reluctantly, he nodded and planted one last, chaste kiss upon her lips. ''You're right. Just got a little carried away with my role. Sorry about that.'' He sighed and rolled onto his back where they both lay side by side and stared at the ceiling. Hoping to diffuse the intensity of the situation, Johnny grinned. ''How about if I make some phone calls, and rustle us up some normal clothes?''

Emmaline nodded and smiled bashfully. ''That sounds like the best idea I've heard in days.''

Monday morning, after two nights in the honeymoon suite at the hotel in Dallas, Emmaline finally felt as ready as she was ever going to be to move into

the Circle BO and begin life as a married couple with
Johnny. Perhaps, she thought with hope as she and
Johnny prepared to check out, she would feel less
overwhelmed by their close proximity after they had
a chance to establish some kind of routine. A routine
that would allow them to live their own lives. To come
and go as they pleased. To stay out of each other's
way.

Because even though he'd treated her with a cool,
somewhat distant reserve during the day, for the past
two nights, when the lights were out, the defensive
walls had crumbled and they'd talked.

And...talked.

More confused than she'd ever been in her life, Emmaline knew that spending too much time in her handsome husband's presence was probably not good for
her staunch sense of reality. Nevertheless she yearned
for the same easy camaraderie they shared at night to
blossom between them during the day. Her rational
mind told her that this was dangerous. But her growing
emotional side couldn't help but wish.

After they checked out of the hotel, their first stop
was the small, furnished apartment Emmaline kept
near the SystaMed labs. They decided that she should
give up her place for now. Once the baby was born,
and her agreement with Johnny was complete, Emmaline would look for a new, larger apartment with a
bedroom she could use as a nursery. Not a clothes-
horse by nature, they were able to pack her sparse
wardrobe into just two suitcases and some boxes.
These meager things, along with a few other scattered
personal effects all fitted into the trunk of Johnny's
sports car.

On the way to the Circle BO from her apartment,

they ducked into a sporting goods store, at Emmaline's insistence. There she bought a comfortable-looking blow-up-type mattress and a hand pump as well. Both items could be stored under Johnny's king-size bed with some spare blankets and pillows, and no one would ever be the wiser.

"You didn't have to pay for that, you know," Johnny informed her, his jaw set with his disapproval when they were once again on the road home. "I promised I'd take care of you and the baby, and I meant it."

"Johnny, I know, but I wanted to. You have already spent more than enough money on me. We're supposed to be business partners, remember? I know that it can never be fifty-fifty with you, financially speaking, but I like to feel as if I'm making some kind of contribution to this project, no matter how small."

"Whatever." Johnny lifted and dropped his shoulder. "I have to admit that I'll probably sleep much better on that air mattress than I have been on the floor."

"Oh, wait a minute. You don't think I bought this for you, do you?" Emmaline was mortified at the thought.

His brows formed a puzzled line. "You bought it for someone else?"

"Yes! Me."

"No way."

"Johnny, I'm not taking your bed from you on top of everything else you're doing for me. It's too much. I couldn't live with myself."

"Oh, please."

Emmaline shook her head. "No, I'm serious. The mattress is for me."

He flexed his grip on the steering wheel. "If you think that I'm going to make a pregnant woman sleep on the floor, then you have another think coming."

Emmaline could see that there would be no arguing with him at the moment, so she wriggled around in her seat and stared out the window at the passing scenery. She would capitulate for now, knowing that there was no way he'd wrestle a sleeping pregnant woman out of her bed, even if it was on the floor.

It was early afternoon by the time they arrived at the ranch and began to move in. Much to Emmaline's relief, none of Johnny's family was home to welcome them as they unloaded her personal effects and carted them up to their suite. Having to greet this mischievous and rabidly curious family after her and Johnny's supposed weekend of wedded passion was something Emmaline preferred to put off as long as possible.

All afternoon they reorganized his bachelor digs, cleaning out his drawers and shelves and closet areas, and making room for Emmaline's possessions. Once they'd finished turning his suite into their suite and figuring out rudimentary morning routines, it was time to once again discuss the subject they'd both ignored and Emmaline had been dreading since the moment she set foot in the room.

Sleeping arrangements.

Unfortunately, in this suite, there was only one bedroom and one bed.

"I wish you'd let me take the air mattress and sleep on the floor," Emmaline protested, when Johnny insisted that she settle her pillows and bedding on his bed.

"Forget it."

"But it really doesn't seem fair, me kicking you out of your bed for an entire year."

Johnny glanced at the bed, deep in thought for a moment. Then, giving his head a sharp shake, he refocused on her. "Listen, you're just going to have to trust me on this, but when you start showing, you're not going to be able to tie your own shoes, let alone get up off that mattress for the dozens of bathroom trips you'll need to make every night." With his pocketknife, Johnny opened the boxes that held the air mattress and the hand pump.

Emmaline settled into a chair she'd dragged to the edge of his bed, put her feet up and sighed. "You sound as though you've been through this process before."

"I have." He grunted, flipping a stubborn staple out of the cardboard. "I've been camping with my sisters-in-law during the last stages of pregnancy, and let's just say it's...an interesting experience. I don't know why they insist on leaving their soft beds and roughing it on the ground, let alone haul themselves out to the woods several times in the middle of the night to do their 'business.' Especially at that stage of the game. But they all do, pregnant or not, every September for the annual Brubaker family camping trip." He waved a dismissive hand at her. "We can skip it this year."

Emmaline swallowed her disappointment. A camping trip with the rowdy Brubaker faction sounded like huge fun. She'd always enjoyed camping out with her various science classes in the past.

However, Johnny was right. She didn't belong at the Brubaker family camp out. Once again, she reminded herself that this was a business deal, not some happy-ever-after love match.

"Maybe your sisters-in-law go camping because the kids love it," she ventured.

Johnny nodded. "Yeah. Probably. Kids can pester the life out of you." He gestured loosely to her midsection with the butt of his pocket knife. "Get ready. Before you know it, junior there, will be harping on you to go camping and a bunch of stuff you've never even dreamed up yet."

Emmaline sighed and shook her head in wonder. "It's hard to believe."

"Believe it." He pulled the mattress out of its box and looked up at her. "But don't stress over it. Kids are a blessing. You're gonna love being a mom." For a moment he paused at his chore, hands propped on his knees, and studied her with a critical eye. "You're going to be a good mom." He tossed the box out of the way. "Damn good."

Even though his words were spoken gruffly and he'd already turned his back on her and refocused on his task, Emmaline tingled at his grudging praise.

But the little jolt of joy didn't last. For some reason, every time Johnny came close to getting at all personal with her, he would withdraw into his shell like a hermit crab. It was so disconcerting.

Emmaline exhaled tiredly. She should count her blessings. Johnny was living up to his end of the bargain. She was a lucky woman. Without him, she couldn't begin to imagine her future.

# Chapter Seven

Before either of them knew it, nearly a month had flown by for Johnny and Emmaline, leaving only eleven months in their agreement. Johnny's family had granted them an unusual amount of space for the past weeks, in a rare effort to give them some privacy. Rather than encourage intimacy, the free time had simply allowed the pseudo newlyweds to bury themselves in their respective work, while they tried to ignore the fact that they slept within a few feet of each other every night.

Which, for Johnny, was murder.

And though the air mattress was far more comfortable than the floor at the hotel in Dallas had been on their wedding night, he still hadn't slept worth beans since the day they'd moved in together.

From where he lay each night, the fragrant smell of her skin, the soft rhythm of her breathing and the quiet murmur of her voice as she bid him good-night had his senses in an uproar. He'd lay there on fire for hours after she'd dozed off. He was going crazy. Sleeping so near her was a torture unlike anything he'd ever experienced.

Never before had Johnny been so bent out of shape over a woman.

It didn't help matters in the least that instead of buying new glasses, she'd opted for contact lenses. She claimed she couldn't believe she'd suffered with such heavy lenses for so many years of her life. Again, the new look in eyewear was more of Patsy's blasted handiwork. As was Emmaline's augmented casual wardrobe. The wardrobe that had him grinding his teeth at night.

Patsy had insisted that Emmaline couldn't live on a ranch and not own a pair of jeans and some cowboy boots. So, soon Johnny noticed his drawers and closet shelves overflowing with Emmaline's new Western wear. It wouldn't have been half so bad if she'd looked in the least bit dowdy or frumpy in the mannish Western garb. But unfortunately that was not the case. She looked cute as a button, her curvy figure blossoming in those ever-tightening jeans and high-heeled boots. And her legs?

Longer than forever.

He hadn't been the only one to notice. He'd seen the looks on the faces of the various ranch hands when she'd come out to the stables to check with him on one thing or another. Dakota and Montana practically climbed over each other to fawn all over her and make her laugh. Nonfamily hands were no better. Raised eyebrows, sly grins, interested smirks, furtive glances. Yeah. They all noticed. They liked what they saw. Johnny couldn't blame them one little bit.

It was enough to pry off the tentative grip he had on his sanity.

Luckily, Emmaline seemed oblivious to the gradual changes in her appearance, and the attention she received from the buffoonish boneheads out in the paddock upon the rare occasion of her visits. Always preoccupied in her own world of science and research, she was no doubt trying to single-handedly cure the world of its hurts. Johnny liked and admired that about her. He liked everything about her. That was the problem.

He was beginning to like her too damn much.

Though they didn't spend much time at all together during the days, the nights were a different story altogether. After lights were out and their room was filled with a milky moon glow that filtered in through his balcony doors, they would talk. Sometimes for hours. Lying there in the gloaming, each in their own bed, they felt free to bare their souls, so to speak. To tell each other stories about their youth and extended family, about their friendships and beliefs and values. To laugh, tell jokes and secrets.

It was almost as if this special time together, spent sharing after dark, wasn't part of reality. Even so, Johnny knew that these intimate sessions were probably not the best idea if they were going to keep this arrangement on a strictly business level. So each day he would head to his frigid shower and renew his vow to give his wife wide berth. To keep his distance, at least until bedtime when, once again, they would stay up half the night talking. His feeble resolve would crumble the moment she shut off the nightstand light and he would find himself captivated by Emmaline's simple charms. Something about her unaffected nature, her lack of phony adornment, her genuine ability to care about her fellow man had Johnny slowly and unconsciously curling around her little finger. The fact that great personal wealth meant nothing to Emmaline or to her family was also incredibly appealing.

To make matters worse, his best-laid plans to steer clear of her were constantly being foiled by his zealous father.

Big Daddy, it seemed, grew fonder of Emmaline with each passing day.

The following Saturday marked four weeks to the day that had sped by since their wedding. To celebrate, Big Daddy decided to throw a Hawaiian luau for the family out under the lanai by the Olympic-size pool. A suckling pig was roasting over a special pit created just for the occasion. Buffet tables on either side of the aromatic spitting and hissing pig were loaded with tropical fruits, exotic salads and baked goods, the likes of which Emmaline had never seen. Servants, dressed in grass skirts and Hawaiian shirts unobtrusively served hors d'oeuvres and fruity drinks.

Potted palm trees, strung with twinkle lights surrounded the pool area and tiki torches burned festively everywhere. An ice sculpture, in the shape of a volcano, oozed some kind of fiery punch that represented molten lava, and—if the red faces of those who sampled this concoction were anything to go by—it was indeed fiery.

Big Daddy had invited Emmaline's parents to join in on the fun of this one-month anniversary celebration, along with all of Johnny's siblings and their spouses and children. Even his cousins, Dakota and Montana were in attendance to celebrate this momentous occasion. All told, the crowd was enormous and not one person was not a bona fide family member. With the exception of Emmaline and her poor unsuspecting parents. Morose and feeling plagued with guilt over this deception, Emmaline followed her faux husband to the wicker love seat of honor, located in the lanai.

She was wearing a flowered sarong-type skirt and top, bare at the midriff and slit to the thigh. Her breasts were pushed up under her chin at what Emmaline felt was an absurd, and most embarrassing, angle. Patsy had insisted she borrow the silly thing and had given her a matching lipstick along with several hothouse orchids that she tucked into her hair. Though it was far more frivolous than was her usual style, Emmaline had to admit that she at least looked festive.

"I feel like such a fraud." She kept her voice low as she settled next to Johnny. Perched awkwardly at his side, she leaned against him and tried to quell her enjoyment of this rare opportunity to play the role of wife.

"Why?"

"You know why." Emmaline could see him glancing around, calculating his audience before reluctantly draping a casual arm over her shoulder and giving her a husbandly squeeze. Somehow, much of the pleasure she felt at his touch was diminished by his hesitant attitude. As he noticed that Mr. and Mrs. Arthur were watching them, he brought his lips to her temple and gave her a little kiss, then, removing his arm, scooted over to his side of the love seat.

Despite the fact that his gesture had been less than enthusiastic, involuntary tingles still danced down Emmaline's neck and shoulders. She glanced at her parents to gauge their reaction. They seemed to buy the act. Good. That was important, considering the rather surprising announcement that she and Johnny planned to make that night.

Emmaline's mother was wearing a giant muumuu over what looked suspiciously like her standard brown-tweed work ensemble. Her chunky brown flats protruded from beneath the colorful ruffle, and even in this July Texas heat, she wore thick coffee-colored support hose. Beads of sweat dotted her red, mottled complexion and her hair was limper than usual.

Emmaline couldn't help but think that Max could do wonders on her mother with a few well-placed snips and a dollop of facial powder. Mrs. Arthur was not an ugly woman. She was simply too busy to care about fashion.

She smiled to herself. Perhaps Patsy was beginning to rub off on her just a little, after all.

Her gaze strayed to her father and Emmaline could see that he was not faring much better than his wife. Damp tendrils of his thinning hair clung to his ruddy cheeks. His only concession to the Hawaiian theme was the lei he wore around his neck. Big Daddy had draped the fragrant orchid necklace over his lumpy, camel jacket when he'd arrived and shoved a glass of molten lava punch into his hands by way of greeting. Both Emmaline's parents now sat together under the lanai. Backs ramrod straight, feet planted firmly on the concrete, they looked distinctly rattled by the boisterous Brubaker family, but struggled to appear to enjoy the chaos for the sake of their only daughter.

"Feel up to limboing later?" He snagged an hors d'oeuvre from a passing tray and gestured to the bar that Big Daddy had set up near the area where the

Hawaiian band would soon be performing. "Big Daddy is holding a competition. I guess, like it or not, we'll have to get out there and put on a show."

"Oh. Sure. I guess we have to do our duty." Disappointment settled like a rock in Emmaline's gut. Oh how she wished that the small acts of affection they performed in public now and then didn't upset him so. In her heart Emmaline knew that she was not the type of woman who could ever make Johnny a suitable wife. Even pretending must be a trial for him. However, they were in this deal together, and if she could endure the next eleven months of playing at marriage, certainly he could, too.

Emmaline found herself looking forward to the limbo contest. She'd never done anything like it before. As a teen, she'd watched the Frankie and Annette and the Gidget beach movies and wondered what it would be like to be so carefree.

Last month, before Dr. Chase's announcement had changed her life forever, had anyone told her that she'd be competing in a limbo contest, she'd have told them they were crazy. Funny how the noisy, fun-loving, completely accepting Brubaker family had brought out the adventurous, carefree side of her personality. A side she hadn't even known existed for twenty-five long years.

Casting a dubious glance at her sweltering parents, she wondered if they would ever learn to simply loosen up and take life a little easier. There were, Emmaline was finding, things in life other than those associated with academia. And, if nothing else came out of this brief union with Johnny Brubaker, she would be thankful for the world of fun his family had introduced to her. She vowed to teach her unborn child, no

matter what his or her IQ, that though learning the
three Rs was important, learning to enjoy life was cru-
cial.

Soon Big Daddy was flapping his arms and whis-
tling for everyone's attention. When silence finally
reigned, and everyone had gathered under the lanai to
crowd around Johnny and Emmaline, the older man
took the opportunity to make a speech.

"Everyone listen up!" This he thundered at his
youngest grandchildren who were still frolicking on
the outskirts of the pool. "Today marks the one-month
anniversary of our newlyweds, Johnny and Emmaline.
And, though I know that their plans to marry came as
a shock to most of us—" a ripple of laughter echoed
across the pool's glassy waters "—I for one, couldn't
be happier. Johnny, my boy, you done good!"

Emmaline saw her mother wince at Big Daddy's
misuse of the king's English.

"Boy, stand up and give us a few words about married life."

Before hauling himself to his feet, Johnny leaned
over to Emmaline and whispered. "I'm gonna tell 'em
you're pregnant now and get it over with, okay?"

Emmaline shrugged and nodded. "Okay." Why
not? They couldn't keep her condition under wraps
much longer. As it was, Patsy's sarong was cutting her
across the middle. No, the truth should come out and
the sooner the better. Emmaline glanced over at her
in-laws. Someday soon she would confess to Big
Daddy and Miss Clarise that the baby was not
Johnny's. They deserved to know that their son was
not a man who would cheat on his fiancée and leave
a strange woman in the family way. Their son was a
kind and loving man who simply wanted the best for

all involved and it was important to Emmaline that they know this about Johnny.

As Johnny cleared his throat, Emmaline cast a covert look at her own parents, her heart accelerating with anticipation and fear. How would they react to the news?

"Well..." Johnny grinned in that casual, sexy Brubaker way that Emmaline thought surely rivaled Elvis in his younger years. His eyes roved over his family's smiling faces as he began his speech. "Marriage isn't so bad, really."

He had to pause, while his brothers and cousins heckled. Finally he continued, in that lazy, cowboy drawl that turned Emmaline's insides to mush.

"And, I guess if you think my marriage to Emmaline was kind of sudden, then you're really gonna go into shock over my next announcement." There was a collective inhalation, then strained anticipation on the part of the entire family as he glanced down at Emmaline.

He pulled her to her feet and tucked her up against his side. Though she knew the gesture was solely for the benefit of those who studied them with curiosity, she was still swept away by the thrill of his warm, gentle touch.

He waited half a beat to build suspense, then launched his bomb. "Emmaline and I are expecting a baby in the spring."

A shrill gasp, then squeals and shrieks of delight went up, filling the early-evening air with strains of joy. Everyone, Emmaline could immediately see, was thrilled.

With the possible exception of her parents, who looked positively stunned to discover that their daughter was not only married, but expecting so soon after. Mrs. Arthur emitted a strangled, gurgling sound from somewhere deep in her throat, and Mr. Arthur gave her knee a reassuring pat. Slowly, as the realization dawned, they rallied, and genuine smiles of delight transformed their stricken faces.

Comments, ribald and otherwise, were tossed about from the crowd. The only indication that Johnny was not perfectly comfortable with such speculation was the fact that he let go of Emmaline's hand to tug at the collar of his colorful Hawaiian shirt.

"I could tell at the wedding that it wouldn't be long before they were in the family way," one of Johnny's brothers shouted.

"Kiss the bride!" another one yelled, and everyone laughed, remembering the last time that suggestion was made.

Johnny shook his head as he was jostled and slapped on the back by well-wishers.

"If you're goin' to do it, hurry it up," Big Daddy harrumphed. "Don't make us wait all day while you stare at her, the way you did at your weddin'."

Again Emmaline could tell by the way the muscles flexed in Johnny's jaw that the obnoxious suggestions that his family foisted upon him grated.

With a reluctance that was obvious only to her, Johnny tugged her to his side and with a few "knock-it-off" waves of his hand at the ogling audience, planted a noisy smacker on her lips.

"Aw, c'mon," Montana yelled. "Give her to me. I can do better than that!"

Everyone laughed.

"Yeah," Johnny drawled, "but this ain't the bedroom and there are kids here."

"Excuses, excuses." Dakota tugged on Emmaline's arm. "Nothin' sexier to me than a pregnant woman." He arched a wolfish eyebrow at Emmaline, who found herself growing embarrassed by the unaccustomed attention. "They glow." Dakota nuzzled her neck and growled, much to the amusement of his relatives.

Johnny, however, was not amused. "I'll thank you to keep your hands to yourself."

It was obvious to Emmaline that it must have been easier for Johnny to simply give in and get it over with as he pulled her none too gently into his embrace. Eyes flashing with his temper, he tilted her chin up with his thumb and forefinger, and gave her the kiss the crowd had demanded. And when he was done, Johnny, looking ever darker, dropped his arms and took a step back. With a clearing shake of his head, he reached out and caught Emmaline just before her knees gave out.

Satisfied, the familial throng turned its attention and listened as Big Daddy outlined the evening's festivities.

"Go ahead and grab a plate. The food is ready. When we're done eatin' we can work off the calories with a little limbo action. After that, the fire dancers will be here to put on a show. When the kids have all been put to bed, the rest of us old fogies can dance cheek to cheek with our beloveds out here on the patio."

Swallowing her disappointment at the tortured look on Johnny's face when Big Daddy mentioned the slow dancing, Emmaline smiled gaily. No one need suspect that her heart was breaking.

# Chapter Eight

Later that night Johnny stood in the shadows on the verandah outside his suite, deep in thought. It was well after midnight. Sprawled out on his bed only a few steps away, Emmaline slept. Pink-cheeked with an exhaustion that had only endeared her further to the Brubaker clan, she'd drifted off over an hour ago. He had to give her credit. She may not have been the most graceful dancer in the family, but her willingness to learn and her insatiable curiosity had once again made her the hit of the party.

Arms propped on the iron balustrade, Johnny leaned over the edge and let his gaze wander over the now-empty pool area at the side of the house where a few lonely tiki torches still burned away the darkness. Images of Emmaline, her body swaying to the soulful strains of the hula music, flitted through his mind. Under the ardent attention of the male members of his family, her usual reserve had crumbled. Emmaline's thousand-watt smile had lit the pool area like one of the flaming torches.

Eyes narrowing, Johnny thought back to the outrageous ways his cousins had flirted with his wife, and he battled an unfamiliar wave of searing jealousy. For pity's sake. She was in the family way. Didn't those idiots have any sense of decency? His brothers had been no better right down to the teenaged Hank. They'd teased and flirted unmercifully with her, praising every awkward wriggle. Completely smitten, Hank had stood plastered to her side as they all took those silly hula lessons.

Even Mr. and Mrs. Arthur had responded to her uncommon zest for life and entered the limbo contest. Mr. Arthur's jacket had finally come off, as had Mrs. Arthur's shoes. And though Johnny wasn't a betting man, he'd lay money on the fact that her parents had managed to enjoy themselves more than they'd care to admit.

Everyone had. Especially his father.

Big Daddy had been in rare form tonight.

For the love of Mike, every time he'd turned around from the moment he and Emmaline had arrived, Big Daddy had goaded him.

"The sun is still a little bright, boy!" Big Daddy shoved a bottle of suntan oil into Johnny's hands. "Better protect that delicate skin." He'd nodded at Emmaline. "Pregnant women are more susceptible to sunburn."

Having no choice, he'd capitulated. The hills and valleys of her incredibly soft and smooth complexion still had his pulses soaring, and that had been hours ago. Johnny rotated his head and shrugged his shoulders in an effort to dispel some of the pent-up tension that lingered.

It would have been bearable if Big Daddy had stopped there. But no. Fate had not been so kind.

"Give Emmaline the lounge chair, son. You sit next to her and rub her feet. Pregnant women like that," his father had told him. Then, a scant half hour later Big Daddy had bellowed, "Johnny, fetch some ice cream for Emmaline, son. Pregnant women go for that. Stick a pickle on the side, just for grins."

"Boy, go give that little gal a smooch from me. She's lookin' kind of lonely, sittin' over there in the corner by herself."

"Son, why doncha rub that darlin' little gal's shoulders for a while? Expectin' women like some extra attention."

Raking a hand through his hair, Johnny stared at the moon. Yeah. His father ought to know what pregnant women would like, having lived through it nine times with his own wife. How could he argue with the voice of experience?

His eyes glazed over.

Though the feel of Emmaline's warm skin was nothing but a memory, it continued to hold him under its spell. Without wanting to seem like the perfect cad in front of those who were enjoying Big Daddy's enthusiastic instruction, Johnny had hugged and caressed and kissed Emmaline over the course of the evening, till he'd feared he'd explode from suppressed desire.

Fingers curling around the iron rail, Johnny fought the urge to punch a hole in the wall. No thanks to his meddling family, he was beginning to fall in love with his wife. And this was not good.

No. Not good at all.

Exhaling heavily, he did a few impromptu push-ups off the rail to burn off some excess energy and to focus on the reasons why falling for Emmaline was such a bad idea.

First and foremost, he had to keep in mind that she was pregnant—with another man's child. Although lately he'd ceased to think of the baby as anything other than his and Emmaline's. Realistically, however, at any moment the creep could come waltzing back into her life and claim what was rightfully his. That alone should scare the holy heck out of him.

But it didn't.

Then, there was the fact that the dirtbag had robbed her of her virginity and then left her feeling inadequate. Now she was suspicious of all men and their motives. Johnny knew Emmaline felt his offer to marry her was done without any thoughts of emotional attachment.

And in the beginning she'd been right.

But now he feared his motives to continue their partnership were changing. An audible groan escaped his throat. Aww, man. His heart was going to get beat to a bloody pulp over this mess. How could she ever trust that his feelings had changed? Become genuine?

Emmaline had trusted a man once before, and she'd been burned. Would she ever be able to open her heart to love again?

The odds were not on his side.

She'd made her position in their arrangement clear from day one. Twelve months only. Strictly business. No hanky-panky. Divorce decree and trust funds to be arranged and finalized by the end of month twelve. Most of the rules in their prenup had been hers, and at the time he'd thought them brilliant.

Now he wasn't so sure.

Aww, hell.

In any event, he could tell by the way she tensed every time he got physical with her that she'd been scarred. Hurt. Betrayed. That she found his touch a repugnant memory of the man that had taken advantage of her.

The fact that he looked so much like the perpetrator who had knocked her up also ate at his gut. A spasm of anger flexed in his jaw. Whenever he thought about the bastard that had ruined her ability to trust, he felt the urge to kill.

Finally deciding that standing outside, doing battle with these demons was pointless, Johnny pushed off the railing and took a deep breath. It was then he heard her cry out, her voice frantic, breathy with fright.

"No...no!"

Rushing to the side of the bed, he could see her thrashing about, as if in the throes of a nightmare.

The sheet was tangled into a ball, and one of his oversize T-shirts was twisted around her body. In the light that filtered in from the moon above and the still-burning tiki torches below, he could see that her eyes were wild, but that she wasn't awake.

"But you promised..."

Arms waving, she found and clutched the front of his shirt as he stood leaning over the bed. Then, with a strength that took him off guard, she yanked him down onto the mattress beside her. Thunderstruck to find himself lying next to her as she flailed, Johnny tried to delicately lever himself away without waking her.

He'd heard somewhere that to wake someone in the middle of a nightmare was not a good idea. It could do some kind of psychological damage. Was that a medical fact or had he been watching too much TV? As his mind searched for the proper procedure for dealing with nightmares, Emmaline grappled with him, grasping and swinging, kicking and clutching.

"Uh," he grunted, trying to pry her fingers out of his hair, "uh, Emmaline?" He dared not speak above a whisper, for fear of traumatizing her. "Emmaline, uh, honey...you are having a bad...dream..." Her hand connected with his jaw. *"Oww...ouch!"*

"Emmaline?" If he could just reach the light on the nightstand, perhaps that would ease her into wakefulness. Unfortunately the light was clear over on the other side of the bed. The button-popping death grip she held on the placket of his shirt prevented him from reaching the switch.

"You blankety-blank...rat fink!"

At long last he found the lamp's switch, and a small pool of light flooded that side of the bed. Squinting against the light, Emmaline bolted upright in bed. Still terror stricken, she blinked, casting her frantic gaze blindly around until reality began to dawn. Then, focusing on Johnny, she reached out and touched him.

He rolled to face her and, still aching from their tussle, propped himself on his elbow.

"Johnny?" It was obvious that she was trying to reckon reality with the world of darkness from which she'd just emerged. Tears fell down her cheeks, and she scrubbed at them with the hem of the sheet.

"Umm-hmm." He peered up at her and rubbed his sore jaw. "You were having a bad dream and I was just trying to check on you."

She could tell that she'd hurt him and reaching out with gentle fingers, touched his reddened jaw.

"Oh, Johnny, I'm so sorry."

"It's all right. I must have scared you, standing there at the edge of the bed, but I heard you crying and I wanted to see— Are you okay?"

"What happened?" With a shaking hand, she plucked at his open shirt, noting the places where the buttons had popped off. "Did I do this, too?"

"Yep. Musta been some kind of nightmare."

Her eyes slid closed and she nodded, beginning to cry all over again.

She looked so forlorn. So lost and alone. Though he knew that reaching for her could be a mistake, he decided to follow his heart nevertheless.

"Hey." He kept his voice low and soothing as he levered himself to a semiupright position. With his free hand he reached out and put his arm around her waist and tugged.

She hiccuped and collapsed against him, allowing herself to be pulled into his embrace. Warm and damp, her cheek pressed into his chest.

"Shh." Still whispering, he stroked her hair. "It was just a bad dream. It's all over now."

"I...I know." Clutching the sheet, she dabbed at her face and heaved a ragged sigh. "You know, I still can't believe I let him touch me."

"How often do you dream about that?"

"All the time. But lately they've been getting worse."

Johnny nodded and brushed her hair back away from her face. He could see the struggle in her eyes and was sorry to learn that she'd been suffering from these recurring dreams.

"I wish there was something that I could do to help."

She scooted a little farther down under the covers and, lifting her cheek from his chest, tentatively reclined against his side. His arm was still circling her waist. "You are. Just by being here."

He shrugged, not feeling much reassured. He wished he had some magic words that would make the night of Chuck and Nora's wedding disappear forever.

"Johnny?" Her voice sounded tiny and high, like a little girl's.

"Hmm?"

"Would you mind if we left the light on for the rest of the night?"

"Mmm. No. Not at all." His eyes slid closed, and suddenly he felt deliciously groggy with Emmaline's warm, sturdy little body leaning against his side.

"Good." She yawned. Soon, Johnny was yawning too. "And, Johnny?" she murmured.

"Hmm?"

"Would you stay with me? And just—" she moistened her lips with the tip of her tongue "—hold me? At least until I fall asleep?"

He was surprised. Surely after that nightmare, the last thing she'd want was a man in her bed. Even one who had not hurt her. Then again, she was frightened. And fright made people do strange things. So did loneliness. And homesickness.

And unfulfilled desire.

Knowing that this was probably not the most brilliant plan of action, he felt powerless to say no. Arms tightening at her waist, he pulled her even more snugly into his embrace as he turned them onto their sides so they could spoon. "Umm-hmm."

"Thank you." The breathy word was filled with contentment.

As he inhaled the sweet, clean scent of her, Johnny had to wonder, as he and his wife drifted off into an exhausted slumber, bodies close, how dull his future was going to be without his Emmaline.

"Come on in."

Big Daddy's voice boomed through the library door to the foyer, where Emmaline stood smoothing her perspiring hands on the stiff denim of her new jeans.

"Are you sure I'm not bothering you?" she asked. "I could come back if you, you know, need to finish what you are doing."

Stepping into the massive library, she gestured to the cigar that Big Daddy was grinding between his teeth as he reviewed the financial section of the newspaper. Her father-in-law was reclining in one of the leather chairs in a comfy grouping. Seated near a wall of windows that overlooked the rolling lawn beyond the mansion's front porch, the area was cozy and private. Perfect for the goal she was here to accomplish.

"No! No, no, honey lamb. You are never a bother to me. In fact I'm glad for the distraction. The stock market is giving me hives these days." He tossed the paper he was reading onto the marble-topped table at his elbow and motioned her to join him in his private, sun-drenched nook.

Her steps stilted, Emmaline made her way across the oak-inlaid floor. She could hear the thundering of her pulse in her ears and hoped that she didn't look as wobbly as she felt.

The time to confess Johnny's innocence to her in-laws was long overdue. Though Johnny did not feel it necessary to explain their private business to anyone, Emmaline couldn't have his parents thinking that their sweet son had been anything but honorable since the day she'd barged into their lives.

"So." Big Daddy's famous grin wreathed his face in wrinkles. "To what good fortune do I owe this unexpected visit from my beautiful new daughter-in-law?" He patted the arm of the chair next to his and waved her over.

As she sank into the overstuffed, luxurious depths, Emmaline wrung her hands and nibbled her lower lip while wondering how to broach a subject that might just get her tossed out of this wonderful family far before she was ready to leave.

Wriggling back into his seat, Big Daddy tucked his chin into his chest and studied her with an expression of compassion that had her throat closing with emotion. "You seem a little nervous, puddin'. What's the problem? You know you can talk to me about anything."

Tears sprang unbidden into Emmaline's eyes. This was going to be much harder than she'd expected. "I...I, uh, I have something to confess to you." Her eyelids fluttered like butterfly wings, attempting to stem the tide that pooled at her lashes. "Something that I should have confessed a long time ago, and now I'm not sure how to go about beginning."

"Mmm." Big Daddy drew on his cigar for a moment. "I know the feelin'. It's the pits, ain't it? Well now, you just go ahead and spit it out and don't worry one bit about how I'll react." A deep chuckle rumbled from within his chest. "After nine kids, I've heard prit'near everything one could confess. And, I'm still alive."

Lip trembling, Emmaline suddenly heard herself blurt, "The baby is not Johnny's." Upon realizing that she'd spoken the dreaded words aloud, she flushed with mortification.

Big Daddy blew a thoughtful string of smoke rings. "Okay, can't say that I've heard that one before. No...no. Not that particular confession. Though Mac had one kind of like it back when his wife was pregnant. But that's a different story..." He waved a stubby hand, scattering the smoke rings. "At any rate, I have a confession of my own to make."

Emmaline stared at him through bleary eyes, her heart pounding, wondering how his confession would affect her fate. "You do?"

"Umm-hmm." His paternal smile was so loving that Emmaline could see without a shadow of a doubt why every one of his nine children worshiped the ground upon which he trod. "My confession is that I can't really say I'm surprised."

"You're not?" It was Emmaline's turn to be surprised.

"Nope. Not really. You see, I know my boy. He never would have cheated on Felicity. But we figured he had his reasons for taking on the responsibility of a relationship with you. He always was big on takin' responsibility. I figure that's why he agreed to marry Felicity in the first place. Felt responsible for the rest of us and our happiness. Didn't occur to me until after they'd broken up that he never loved her." Big Daddy's wink was knowing. "Leastwise, not the way he loves you."

"Oh, Big Daddy." Shoulders slumped, face cradled in her hands, Emmaline let the tears flow. A crisp, clean handkerchief the size of a small tablecloth was pressed onto her knees, and through her hiccuping sobs Emmaline could hear the old man's soothing murmurs.

"There, there, now, little honey lump. No reason to cry. But, if it makes you feel better, you just go on ahead. My sweet wife cried through all nine of her pregnancies, it seemed. That's why I still carry them big hankies."

"Johnny doesn't love me."

Big Daddy chuckled. "Wish I had a nickel for every time I heard a woman in the family way say that about her husband. Now you just forget such crazy talk. My boy loves you. No question. I can see it, and I'm a bit of an expert on the way a man loves his wife."

Not seeing the sense in arguing with the well-meaning patriarch of the Brubaker clan, Emmaline simply sent him a watery smile and dabbed at her eyes. "Johnny doesn't want you to know. He wants you to think the baby is his."

"As far as I'm concerned, it is his."

"You don't mean that."

"Oh, but I do."

Emmaline choked back a sob. She didn't deserve such a wonderful man for a father-in-law. "I am so sorry that we didn't tell you the whole story from the beginning."

"Like I said, sweetheart, we know you had your reasons, and the missus and I guessed they must have been pretty painful. We saw the stress you were under on the day we met. But I want you to know one thing from the get-go. To me, and to my wife, that little baby you're carryin' is just as much one of my grand-babies as any of the rest of 'em, and that's the honest truth. A Brubaker through and through. As far as I'm concerned, this little child is yours and Johnny's and the details that brought you two together are none of my affair. You're together. He loves you. You love him. He's thrilled about the baby. That's all that matters.''

Emmaline paused and studied her father-in-law's face, noting the high color in his cheeks and the suspicious twinkle in his eye.

"You knew all along, didn't you?" she whispered.

Eyes wide, Big Daddy drew his chin into his neck and blinked up at her, his face the picture of innocence. "Knew what, honey pie?"

"That we married for the sake of the baby. That's why you have pushed Johnny's attentions on me from the beginning, isn't it?" A smile tickled the corners of her lips. "Telling him to wait on me hand and foot and encouraging him to kiss me every time he turns around because, and I quote here, 'pregnant women like that.'''

Big Daddy shrugged and puffed on his cigar. "Sometimes true love needs a little nudge in the right direction, know what I mean?"

"And that's why you stopped by our honeymoon suite, the morning after the wedding, isn't it? To check up on us."

"Just wanted to make sure you hadn't decided to run off. The minute I set eyes on you, I knew you'd make a fine daughter and the perfect wife for my boy."

"Oh, Big Daddy. I'm far from perfect for Johnny."

"Sweetheart, why don't you just let him be the judge of that?"

With that probing question Big Daddy stabbed out his cigar in a crystal ashtray, stood and walked to her side. Bending over, he planted a noisy kiss at her temple, ruffled her hair and, with a parting murmur of endearment, left the library.

Too overcome with emotion to respond, Emmaline could only sit there and cry. Whether she was crying from happiness or melancholy would probably take her the rest of her natural life to figure out.

# *Chapter Nine*

The lazy days of summer were anything but.

Consumed with her work in the lab and the mental gymnastics of trying to keep Johnny at an emotional arm's length, Emmaline was amazed to find the calendar pages swiftly flipping through the month of August and rolling into the middle of September. She could scarcely believe that she was already halfway through her pregnancy.

A daily routine had evolved of late, and Emmaline was finally beginning to settle into the role of married woman and expectant mother. Down at SystaMed, all the girls were envious of her handsome husband, though clearly stymied as to how Emmaline had managed to land that particular fish. Whenever Johnny would drop by to take her to lunch, as he was doing today, the twitters of appreciation could be heard echoing up and down the hallway as he passed.

''Your hunky hubby is here to pick you up.'' Nora's whisper was teasing as Johnny ambled toward her workstation. "Mmm-mmm, honey. You are one lucky gal. I can see why he caught your eye at my wedding. You're just lucky I didn't spot him at my reception, because I'd have stolen a dance for sure. And maybe a kiss for the bride." She wiggled her brows. "If he wasn't your husband and my husband's boss, I'd be flirtin' with him for sure. Love those cowboys."

Nora still didn't know that Johnny was not Ronny Shumacher, man of mystery and father of her unborn child, and Emmaline didn't feel any need to enlighten her.

As Nora whistled her appreciation for Johnny under her breath, Emmaline felt the fire steal into her cheeks. She batted her friend on the arm. "Really, Nora, you are a married woman."

"Yeah, but I ain't dead," Nora deadpanned under her breath, then sauntered away. "Hi, Johnny."

"Hey, Nora." He returned her breezy wave, then bent to kiss Emmaline's lips. "Hi, honey."

The women in the research department's laboratory where she worked all sighed. The men snorted and rolled their eyes at the women.

"Hi." Her waistline burgeoning, Emmaline felt that compared to everyone else in the room she was about as attractive as a buffalo and half as graceful.

"Ready for lunch?" His breath tickled the back of her neck as he spoke, his low tones meant just for her. Gently his hands caressed her shoulders and neck, rubbing the day's tensions away.

"Uh, yeah. Sure." Though she knew he was only touching her this way for the benefit of her interested co-workers, Emmaline couldn't help but enjoy his ministrations.

"Shall we?" With extreme gallantry, he assisted

her out of her chair. Then, tossing a nod of acknowledgment to the lab's watchful staff, he began to fill her in on his plans for their lunch. "I packed a picnic basket and thought we could sit out behind the lab near the pond since I don't have much time."

"That would be lovely," she murmured. A multitude of smiling glances followed their progress to the door and beyond, and Emmaline could still feel her department watching even as they crossed the lawn and settled in at the picnic table near the pond. A giant willow tree protruded from the bank, its graceful branches trailing on the ground and hanging over the water. It afforded them the perfect amount of privacy.

"You look beautiful today." Johnny studied her face, a tender smile gracing his lips.

Flustered, Emmaline ducked her head and began unloading the picnic basket. "They can't hear us out here. You don't have to say that."

"But I do. It's true, you know."

"Oh, balderdash." A grudging smile tugged at her lips and she glanced shyly up at him. He was teasing. Wasn't he? "I'm as puffy as a marshmallow. You should see my feet. Fred Flintstone has nothing on me."

"You don't look puffy to me. You look beautiful."

"Would you stop?"

"Why?"

"Because."

"Why can't a man tell his wife that she's beautiful?"

Emmaline shrugged as she loaded their plates with food. "Because I don't look beautiful. That's why."

"Yes, you do. You are a lovely woman, Emmaline. Inside and out. Patsy's hair and wardrobe makeover made it a little more obvious, that's true, but lately you seem to radiate happiness. Confidence. A special glow. It's very appealing. Sexy.''

His piercing stare was unnerving and caused her heart to flutter wildly beneath her breast.

"I thought people told pregnant women they glowed to keep them from feeling sorry for themselves.''

"Do you feel sorry for yourself?''

"No." She had to admit that when Johnny looked at her that way, she felt beautiful. "Quite the contrary. You are right. I'm happy these days. Very happy.''

"Me, too.''

Whether from the fact that he wasn't locked in a loveless marriage with Felicity, or because he was beginning to enjoy her company, Emmaline couldn't tell. And because this was such an idyllic moment, one that she would treasure for the rest of her life, she didn't care to know the reason for his happiness. The fact that they were both happy in the here and now was enough for her. The fact that Johnny thought she was beautiful didn't hurt matters any, either.

When the day finally came for her twenty-week prenatal checkup, Emmaline asked Johnny for a ride into town, since her aging compact car had been acting up of late.

And, seeing that this was the week of the infamous annual September Brubaker camping trip, asking anyone else was impossible. The house was empty, as the entire Brubaker family and staff had answered the call of the wild. Pickup trucks loaded with tents and sleeping bags and fishing poles and enough hampers of hamburgers to feed an army had caravanned down the driveway early that morning and would not return until private school started for the kids next week.

As much as everyone had cajoled them, trying to convince them to join in on the fun, Johnny had remained firm. He and Emmaline were staying home. Though everyone had winked and smiled and teased about giving the newlyweds some space, Emmaline knew that Johnny had other reasons for keeping them home.

She wasn't part of the family. Never would be. No use building painful memories that his family would have to overcome on future camping trips. And, as much as she hated the idea of missing out on what promised to be a rollicking week of family fun, Emmaline had to admit that some quiet time spent with Johnny held a forbidden appeal that had her toes curling at the thought. Even a trip to the doctor took on the quality of a special occasion when Johnny came along.

Dr. Chase's effervescent nurse greeted them warmly when they arrived at the clinic. Before Johnny could protest, she ushered them both into the examination room.

"Sorry about that." Emmaline glanced over at him after the nurse had weighed her and taken her blood pressure, then disappeared. "I guess she just figured you'd want to be here for the ultrasound."

Eyes roving around the walls, Johnny took in the various posters that graphically depicted the miracle of childbirth. "Uh-huh." Seeming to not quite know what to do with himself, he settled into the visitor's chair in the corner and searched for a spot to plant his gaze. He glanced up at her face. "You okay with me being here?"

She giggled. "Of course."

"I could leave."

"Please don't." Realizing she may have sounded a little too dependent upon his company, she explained. "Dr. Chase would probably think it strange if you took off now. Don't you think?"

He hunched his shoulders. "Oh, sure. Okay. Just wondered. I thought maybe you'd want some privacy, to you know, take off your clothes, or you know…" His gaze darted to the floor. "I don't know much about how these women's things work."

A warm blush suffused her cheeks. How silly for her to feel so awkward around him. After all, they'd shared a room now, since the middle of June. Then again, they'd always done their dressing in the privacy of the bathroom.

"I don't think I'll have to strip down for an ultrasound. I mean, it's the baby he's interested in. Not me."

"Oh. Sure. I just, you know…"

Her heart rolled over at his lopsided, rather vulnerable smile. He was such a generous man. In so many ways. "I know, and you're very sweet."

Their gazes connected for an intense moment. Though she knew he resisted such displays of emotion toward her, they'd shared many more of these electric glances than either of them cared to admit since her nightmare, back in the middle of July. Over the past weeks, when the dreams got rough, Johnny would climb up into bed beside her and—with a few whispered words and a comforting arm around her middle—she would relax and fall back to sleep. More often than not after such an episode, Johnny himself would fall asleep, only to wake up next to her the following morning. She loved those sweet times in his sleepy embrace.

Their poignant moment of eye contact was suddenly shattered by the jovial Dr. Chase's entrance. Bursting through the door, he pumped first Johnny's hand and then Emmaline's.

"You're looking well, Emmaline," the older man commented with a smile. "Marriage and pregnancy certainly seem to agree with you. She positively glows, doesn't she, Papa?"

Without waiting for a response, the doctor grabbed Emmaline's chart, scanned the notes the nurse had made and with a satisfied nod, had her lie back on the table. As he lifted her blouse and tucked it up under her bra and lowered the elastic band at her waist, he grinned at Johnny.

"Well, Papa, what do you want? A boy, or a girl?"

Again Johnny searched for a place to land his gaze other than his wife's smooth, gently rounded belly. "I...uh..."

"Don't care, huh?" Chuckling, Dr. Chase grabbed a bottle of some kind of lotion and, without bothering to warm it up, squirted it all over Emmaline's stomach. The good doctor ignored her gasp. "That's a good way to be." With a frown, he reached over his patient and adjusted the dials on the ultrasound equipment. "Want to find out the sex, or do you two want to be surprised?"

Johnny's gaze shot to Emmaline and his expression announced that he hadn't given it much thought. So far, Emmaline knew he hadn't really considered the baby in anything other than abstract terms. The fact that there was a little person in Emmaline's womb was at this point, anyway, still beyond his ken. She knew

how he felt. With the exception of the occasional
nudge or flutter beneath her navel, most of the time
she was convinced that the past few months were simply a dream.

"I'd like to know," Emmaline volunteered, with a
questioning glance at Johnny.

He nodded and gave her a "why not" shrug.

"Okey-dokey," Dr. Chase boomed. "You know,
the way I look at it, it doesn't matter when you find
out. It's always a surprise, no?" With his remote unit,
he began to scan her belly, and suddenly the skeletal
image of a tiny baby filled the screen. "Hmm..."
Deep in thought, Dr. Chase moved the remote here
and there, pressing, measuring and making the occasional comment for the benefit of his audience. "As
you can see," he murmured, "this is the baby's
spine."

Rising to his feet, Johnny took the few steps necessary to reach Emmaline's side, and wearing an idi-
otic grin, he leaned over her forearm to peer at the
screen. "Well, for Pete's sake. There's a little person
in there. You can see that clear as day, can't you?"

He glanced down into Emmaline's face with such
an expression of awe and reverence it made the back
of her throat swell and burn.

"Yeah." Dr. Chase grunted. "And down here we
have the head." With the quick push of some buttons,
he measured the baby's skull from front to back.
"Looks good...and over here you can see the
hands...oh, look, Daddy, baby is waving at you...."

Eyes suspiciously bright, and his voice high and
tight with raw emotion, Johnny whispered, "Hey
there, little one."

Emmaline swallowed a sob. Tears spilled from the

corners of her eyes and ran into her ears. There was no one on this earth with whom she'd rather be sharing this moment than Johnny Brubaker.

"This is the baby's stomach...up here, the heart. You can see it beating...over here are the kidneys. Let's see...femur bone...and there's the other one." Dr. Chase took another quick measurement. "Looking good...there are the feet, you can even make out the toes if you look closely...and...hmm...back up here...hmm...hmm...well, I don't see anything here."

Fearing her heart had stopped beating, Emmaline shot a frantic glance at Johnny. Something was missing? Was something wrong with the baby?

Johnny grasped her hand and looked as stricken as she felt.

"Uh, Dr. Chase, what do you mean, you...uh... don't see anything?" he asked.

Dr. Chase shrugged. "Just that. Nothing there. I'm not 100 percent positive, of course, but if you wanted to paint the nursery pink, I think you'd be okay."

It was a girl? Emmaline smiled with relief and wonder, then looked up at Johnny to gauge his reaction. Miraculously, he looked as thrilled as she felt.

"It's a *girl!*" He crowed in jubilation and, squeezing Emmaline's hand, brought it to his lips for a kiss. Then, in an impulsive gesture, he leaned down and kissed her hard, on the mouth. "It's a girl!" he whispered against her lips, "and she is as beautiful as her mother."

At that moment, as his shining gaze flashed his happiness and excitement into hers, Emmaline knew for sure that she was in love. And not just with the baby in her belly or the wonderful world at large. But with the handsome, sweet, caring man whose eyes beamed his sudden and genuine happiness over the little life in her womb.

Later that afternoon—as they sat together in a booth in the back of their favorite coffee shop sharing a piece of pie and reviewing the pile of baby-naming books and other "what to expect" type literature that Johnny had insisted they purchase on the way home from the doctor's office—Emmaline began to have doubts. The more she read, the more helpless and unempowered she began to feel. Surely finding the cure for cancer was easier than raising a baby.

"You know—" Johnny's nose was buried in what boasted to be the hippest, hottest baby-naming book on the market "—I think we'd have been better off going to the music store and getting a copy of the Top 100 Country Chart. I mean, since we're going to name the baby after a country-western singer, that would probably be the best place to start."

Emmaline's heart turned over and her eyes stung. He wanted to name the baby in the Brubaker family tradition? How incredibly touching. She battled back the tears that seemed to hover at the brink of her lashes all the time these days. Swallowing hard, she took a deep breath before daring to speak.

"Uh, what did you have in mind for a name?"

Johnny leaned back against the squeaky red plastic of the booth and darted a pensive gaze at the whirring blades of the ceiling fan. "Well, a lot of the good names have already been taken by my brothers and sister. Wynonna and Naomi are Bru's twins. And Buck's got one named LeAnne. Patsy's got Crystal Gayle." He tucked his chin into his shoulder and looked askance at her. "Nobody has taken Dottie yet."

"Dottie?"

"After Dottie West."

"Yes, I know."

"You don't like it?"

"Well, doesn't it sound just a little...dotty?"

Johnny grinned. "I guess. How about Dolly?"

"Too...I don't know."

Johnny chuckled. "Whatever we name her, she'll be beautiful. I know. I've seen her."

Again, the familiar lump crowded into Emmaline's throat. "I don't care. You pick a name."

"How about Rosanne?"

"Rosanne? That's pretty. Why did you pick that?"

His smile was bashful, and a spark of what Emmaline could only figure was hope flashed behind his eyes. "Because that's what Johnny Cash named his daughter."

"Oh." Unable to hold back the tears, Emmaline plucked a fistful of napkins from the dispenser. After dramatically blowing her nose, she flopped forward on the Formica table and gave vent to the bittersweet emotion that crowded her throat.

"You don't like it?"

"I...I..." she blubbered, "I think it's the prettiest name I ever heard."

His grin of delight only made her cry harder.

Since even the kitchen staff had vacated the premises for the annual camp out, Johnny ran into town that evening to pick up some Chinese food. When he returned, loaded down with fragrant bags, he found Emmaline sitting at a table near the fountain in the rose garden. It was difficult to tell which was leaking more, Emmaline or the fountain. Watery-eyed, puffy-cheeked, red-nosed and sniffing into a soggy tissue, she was—with the exception of her chic hairstyle— just as disheveled and goofy-looking as the day they'd met. His heart melted. To him she was the most beautiful girl in the world.

Her smile wan, she lifted a hand in greeting. "Hi."

"Hi."

He hadn't thought it was possible to care for her any more than he did earlier that day in the doctor's office. But she seemed to just find new and endearing ways to fill the empty corners of his heart with every grain of sand that passed through the hourglass.

Concern tightened his face. Surely she couldn't still be bawling over the fact that he wanted to name the baby Rosanne. He ambled down the brick path and set the bag on the table.

"Emmaline?"

"Hmm?"

"What's wrong?"

"Oh...nothing."

"C'mon. You can't fool me. Something's up. Spill it."

The fact that she looked over at the bag of food with interest was a good sign.

"What'd you get?" She dabbed at her nose with a fresh tissue.

"Sesame beef. Chicken almond chow mein. Barbecue pork. Fried rice. And, some kind of spicy cashew shrimp thing."

"Umm." Fingers fluttering, she motioned for him to push the bag closer so that she could see.

"Okay. But," he said, digging into the bag and

withdrawing the warm cartons, "you have to promise
to tell me what's wrong."

As he spread out the feast and unwrapped the chop-
sticks, Emmaline tried to rein in her emotions and explain. A too-bright smile lifted her lips. She filled her
lungs with a giant gulp of air and plunged ahead.

"Well, I guess it all started when I realized—"
blinking rapidly, she paused to regroup "—when
I...when I...realized...that the—" She waved the tissue in the air and allowed her head to drop back on
her shoulders.

"Yes?" he encouraged.

"That the...the...baby is..." She hiccuped and
covered her hand with her mouth for a moment.

"Uh-huh." He was trying not to pressure her, but
for crying in the night, the suspense was killing him.

"...the baby is...real." A giant, racking sob had her
shoulders bobbing.

"Oh, honey." Johnny moved to her side, sat down
next to her and gathered her into his arms. He knew
how she felt. The reality of the baby had taken him
off guard, too. "I know."

"No! You don't know!"

Okay. He lifted a shoulder in an affable shrug. No
use arguing with her in this condition.

"Johnny, I don't think I can do this!" She blubbered and gestured helplessly at the pile of books and
information she'd spent most of the day reading. "I'm
not kidding! I don't know anything about babies! I
don't think I've ever even held one! How on earth am
I going to know what to do when she cries?"

"Just pick her up."

She bestowed him with a beleaguered look. "Then
what?"

"Well, there are usually three or four things that make 'em cry." With her nestled against his side, he pulled her head to his shoulder and, crossing his ankles, stared unseeing at the spray of water that shot into the air from the statue in the fountain.

"But I don't know what those things are!" Her cry was plaintive. "Now, ask me about inhibiting the migration of cancer cells and...well, I can hum a few bars."

Johnny chuckled and kissed the top of her head. "Stop worrying. I don't think any of my sisters-in-law knew much about babies when they started their families, and so far their kids are thriving." He held up a finger. "Okay, first you check to see if they need a diaper change. If that's not it, try to feed 'em or burp 'em. If that's not it, they are probably tired, so sit down and rock 'em till they doze off."

"You make it sound so easy." She sniffed.

"That's because it is. Lots of people do it. Millions. Billions. Emmaline, you are going to be a great mom. A wonderful mom. An A-plus, superachieving mom."

"But how do you know?"

"Because I know you. Honey, there isn't anything you can't do when you put your mind to it. I'm constantly amazed by what goes on up here." He gave a gentle tap on her forehead.

It was true. Though he found Emmaline as cute as a button physically, it was what went on upstairs that really turned Johnny on. He'd never met a woman who could captivate his attention the way she could. She was savvy. Sharp. Witty. Sweet and loving. All the Girl Scout virtues. Just what he'd always wanted in a wife.

"Really?" She sounded more like a lost little kid,

needing assurance from her father, than a renowned scientist hot on the trail of one of this century's biggest discoveries.

"Mmm. Really."

Her sigh was ragged. "Johnny?"

"Yeah?"

"After we, you know…after I…me and the baby… when we move out…"

Johnny's heart clutched. He could barely stand to contemplate the day. "Yeah?" He hoped he didn't sound as sick at heart as her words made him feel.

"If I have a question about…uh, little Rosanne, could I call you?" She looked up at him with hope in her eyes. "And, you know, run a few questions by you?"

"Of course. I'd be mad if you didn't."

"Good." She smiled with relief. "And, Johnny?"

"Hmm?"

"Would you come over, if I really needed help and my mom was out of town?"

"In a hot New York second."

Sighing, she nestled back against his shoulder. "And, Johnny?"

"Yep?" Again his heart stopped for a beat. He couldn't take much more of this talk about her and Rosanne living apart from him and his family.

"Could you pass me the spicy shrimp thing?"

He threw back his head and laughed. "You must be feeling better."

She nodded and struggled to sit up. "Much."

Much later that night, after they'd both retired to their respective beds, Emmaline tried to drift off but couldn't. No longer able to sleep on her stomach, she tossed and turned, looking for a comfortable position. Finally giving up, she hung over the edge of the bed and peered through the dark to the shadowy lump that was her husband.

"Johnny? You awake?"

"Yep."

"Me, too."

"I know. You're thrashing around like a kite in a thunderstorm."

"Sorry."

"No, it's okay. I can't sleep, either. Keep thinking about that tiny little spine."

Emmaline propped herself on her elbow and grinned. "Wasn't that awesome?"

"A miracle." His voice held a note of pure wonder.

"You know, since last week, I can feel her move almost every night when I lie down."

His covers rustled. "Really?"

"Umm-hmm. And, sometimes after I eat."

"What's it feel like?"

"Oh, little thumps. She's been pretty active tonight. Must have something to do with having her picture taken."

"Is she doing it now?"

Emmaline ran her hand down to her stomach. "Here and there. She will kick a little, then rest." Leaning over the edge of the bed, she tried to make out his face in the moonlight. "Want to feel?"

"Could I?"

He made no attempt to suppress his interest as he wrestled back his covers and scrambled out of his bed. Before her grin could reach from ear to ear, he was tucked in bed beside her, his hand pawing through the covers searching for the little bulge that was Rosanne.

"Hey, little baby," he crooned in her ear.

"You're a little high," Emmaline said, her voice droll as he cupped her breast.

"Oops! Sorry!" He sounded anything but contrite and his laughter was contagious.

"You did that on purpose!" Emmaline accused, giggling. It was a relief to know that such an intimate touch did not cause her to recoil. She'd wondered about that. Ronny's parting shot still echoed in her ears, reminding her of her lack of sex appeal.

Johnny did his best to sound wounded. "I did not!"

"Did, too." Grabbing his groping hand, she redirected it to her belly. "There. Now. Sit still and wait. She'll be around in a minute."

"Okay."

His contented sigh tickled the hairs at her nape. They lay back against the pillows, locked together like pieces of a puzzle and waited for the baby to move.

"I don't think she's really moving at all." His sexy voice was low and teasing. "I think this is just a ploy to get me into your bed."

"In your dreams," Emmaline quipped, but her pulse raced and her blood literally sang through her veins.

"I've had a few, yes."

Again there was a playful quality in his voice that she decided not to take seriously. She searched her brain for another, safer topic of conversation. "You know, Patsy said to me, just before they left to go camping this morning, that I sure was big for only three months along."

Johnny laughed. "She never has missed a trick."

"She wondered if it was twins. She told me that twins run in the family."

"What did you tell her?"

"I told her that you'd simply been feeding me too well."

"Oh, right. Blame it on me."

"Well, she said that you looked like you'd put on a few pounds, too."

"Hey!" This time he did sound truly wounded. Rising up on his side, he pressed his nose against hers. "I'll have you know that I'm still in peak condition for a man my age."

She'd noticed. But she wasn't going to tell him that.

"Man," he griped, miffed at his sister, "that is one cold woman. I don't know how Justin puts up with her."

"He loves her."

"Yeah." Johnny sighed against her lips. "Love. Makes a monkey out of a man."

It didn't take much change of position for him to close his mouth over hers, and as he rolled her onto her back and deepened the kiss, Emmaline thought she might just explode with the sweetness of it all. Through the kiss his hand remained planted firmly, possessively on her belly. She wound her hands around his neck and arched instinctively against him, and his groan filled her mouth. Adrenaline coursed through her veins and into Rosanne's, and soon the small baby was kicking Johnny's hand.

Smiling against her mouth, Johnny whispered, "I think she wants to know my intentions."

Emmaline's lips curved with his. "And those are?" She had to admit she was more than a little curious herself. Slowly Johnny's caring touch was helping to heal the scars that Ronny had left. Could Johnny really find her appealing? There was certainly no one here to perform for....

Reluctantly he moved away from her body and settled on the mattress next to her. "Mmm, not for her young ears, I'll tell you that right now."

She shivered at his words.

"I'm sorry. You're shaking. I shouldn't have done that." Lightly he trailed his fingertips across her lower lip and then blew the air out of his lungs in a frustrated huff. "I shouldn't have said that."

"It's okay." Emmaline wanted to scream with frustration. She closed her eyes and once again Ronny's words echoed in her mind. *I doubt that a spinster like you could ever satisfy a real man.*

His prophecy must be true. For it seemed that every time she got close to getting intimate with Johnny, he would back off.

Why, oh, why couldn't she seem to remember that this was a blankety-blank business deal? The sooner she got that through her blankety-blank head, the better. To him, she was simply a "get out of jail free" card from his commitment to Felicity.

Again the baby kicked, and Johnny chuckled. "So you want to know my intentions, huh, kiddo?"

Bending at the waist, Johnny leaned over her and brought his mouth to Emmaline's belly. "Well, my little rosebud, when you are big enough, I'm going to teach you how to ride a horsey. Doesn't that sound like fun? And I'll teach you how to ride a bike and drive a car and, well, all the major transportation education will be my territory." He stroked Emmaline's stomach, much the way he would pat and comfort a baby. "And of course I'll beat up all the guys who try to ask you out on a date."

Even as she tried to steel her heart and remember that this was a marriage in name only, his sweet murmurings to the baby had Emmaline's heart melting into a puddle of mush. Could she really survive eight more months of this mentally torturous marriage?

As if on cue, Rosanne thumped Johnny's hand, and he laughed out loud. "She's one tough cookie, this one."

"I think it's my soaring blood pressure that has her all in a dither," Emmaline confessed, trying to affect a breezy attitude. Perhaps if she brought how he made her feel when he touched her out in the open, it wouldn't seem so taboo. Perhaps if they could talk about her adolescent crush, he could help her get over it.

"I'm not used to this kind of...excitement." She peered at him, studying the nuances of his reaction.

"Ah. Of course. I should have thought of that. Are you..." He sounded genuinely concerned. "Are you okay?"

"Fine."

"I know that you probably have some unhappy memories about the baby's father. I'm sure that my pawing at you, even jokingly, isn't helping matters."

So. He was joking. Her heart thudded dully beneath her breast.

"Actually, there wasn't all that much to remember," she confessed, fighting the flames of mortification that licked at her cheeks. "It all happened so quickly, it's a bit of a blur. To be honest, I don't really remember that much about that night. It's, uh, the next morning that sticks out in my mind."

"Why is that?"

Emmaline cast her gaze to her hands. "Because that's when he told me that he...that I..."

She felt unbelievably foolish discussing her ignorance about lovemaking to Johnny, especially in light of the fact that she was four months pregnant. But it was true. The brief encounter with Ronny and the few kisses she'd shared with Johnny were really the extent of her experience. And, according to Ronny, her tentative forays into sexual waters were nothing to brag about.

"Yes?" Johnny's gaze was patient and kind.

"Well, I'm not much of a lover, I guess." She donned a mask of false bravado and laughed a tinny laugh.

Johnny stilled, not speaking for a long time. So long, in fact, that Emmaline began to wonder if her confession had somehow offended him.

When he finally spoke, there was an odd mixture of steeliness and possessiveness in his voice. Rolling onto his side, he propped his head on a pillow and she could feel him scrutinizing her through the darkness.

"That guy really did a number on you, didn't he?"

Emmaline shrugged. "Yes and no."

"What do you mean?"

"Well, I don't really know how badly he damaged me, because as far as I know, he could be telling the truth."

Mutely Johnny shook his head. "No. No, he's a damn liar."

Emmaline's gaze collided with his. "Really?"

"Really. And if this wasn't a marriage in name only, I'd prove it to you right now."

Her eyes slid closed, and Emmaline silently cursed the day they'd come up with that stupid contract.

# Chapter Ten

"Johnny?" Pushing herself upright in bed, Emmaline peered groggily at the hour as it glowed red in the darkness from the nightstand. *"Johnny?"* This time she raised her voice, hoping to wake him. She could tell he was sleeping soundly by the deep timbre of his snore. Unable to roust him out, she grabbed a pillow off the bed and hurled it at his head. *"Johnny!"*

"Huh? Wha—?"

"Johnny, I think it's time."

Still half-awake, he shot upright on his air mattress and fumbled above his head for the light on the nightstand. "Already?"

"Well, I was due last week."

She could scarcely believe that herself. Where had the time gone? The second half of her pregnancy had zoomed by even more quickly than the first. Baby showers, shopping trips, layettes, bassinets, baguettes, doughnuts, ice cream, weight gain, new maternity clothes, leave of absence from work—it had all been a blur.

Only the moments spent with Johnny alone, whispering in the darkness, were suspended in time. Branded in her memory for life. Somehow, in spite of their best intentions to keep this a simple business deal, a bond had been forged. At least she felt the bond. Even if he didn't.

Another mild contraction hit, and Emmaline practiced the deep-breathing techniques that she and Johnny had learned in one of their myriad birth classes, down at the hospital.

After rubbing the sleep from his eyes, Johnny scrambled up onto the bed and took her hand. Together, they hoo-hoo-hee'd until Emmaline felt the pain begin to ebb.

"Good girl. Okay." Johnny glanced at his wrist. No watch. He looked rattled. "How far apart are the contractions?"

"About five minutes. Maybe a little more."

"Oh, boy."

Emmaline could sense his trepidation. He wasn't ready for this. So what if they'd taken all the classes and practiced the hoo-hooing and the hee-heeing till they'd both begun to hyperventilate. This was the real thing. He wasn't ready for the real thing. Neither was she.

"Okay, baby." With a final pat to her very pregnant belly, Johnny launched himself off the bed and proceeded to stumble and fumble around the room in an effort to get dressed and locate his watch and keys. "Daddy is doing his best. Don't get too excited."

A smile threatened to curve her lips even through the pain. For whatever reason, ever since Johnny had given a name to the baby, he'd referred to himself as Daddy. It was a touching gesture. She only wondered how long that would last after their marriage had dissolved. No doubt it would all be over once he met Miss Right and began having children with her. Shoving the niggling worries to the back of her mind, she concentrated on making it through another contraction.

"You okay?"

"Uh-huh." She exhaled long and slow. "Relax. We have time."

"Good, good. Time is good." Finally dressed with his boots on the correct feet, he strode to the bed and gathered Emmaline into his arms.

"What are you doing?"

"Taking you to the hospital."

"I can walk."

He set her back down on the bed and raked a hand over his shadowed jaw. "Oh."

"You carry the suitcase. I'll carry me. Meet you at the car in two minutes."

"Good. Taking the car is good."


"She sure looks like you, Johnny," Patsy crowed, peering over her brother's arm into the tiny, wrinkled face of the newly born Rosanne Cash Brubaker.

"Spittin' image!" Big Daddy's face glowed red with pride. "Right, sugar doll?"

Miss Clarise nodded. "It's uncanny. I'll have to dig out your baby pictures, honey," she murmured, touching Johnny lightly on the arm. "You won't believe the resemblance."

Another word and Emmaline was sure Johnny's buttons would burst right off his shirt, perchance injuring someone in the process. Never in her life had

she ever witnessed the love, the pride, the fierce pos-
sessive streak that had surfaced in Johnny the instant
Rosanne was born. Unless they decided to announce
that Johnny was not the biological father to anyone
other than his parents, no one would ever be the wiser.
The birth certificate already sported his bold signature.

Reclining on the hospital's birthing bed, Emmaline
watched as the in-laws who had arrived so far crowded
around her daughter. She wondered, with a contented
sigh, when Johnny would allow anyone else to hold
the baby. Including herself. At some point she was
going to have to learn to nurse the little thing. Unless,
she thought with a groggy smile, Johnny was planning
on taking over that particular chore as well.

She glanced at the clock. Her parents should arrive
any minute. No doubt her mother would want to hold
the baby. After that, the rest of Johnny's family would
surely filter in to have a peek. A blissful smile stole
across her face.

Oh, well. There would be plenty of time to hold
Rosanne later.

For now the child was in good hands.

Since the moment the squalling, red-faced, dark-
haired little angel had emerged from the womb, baby
Rosanne had been in Johnny's sole possession. And,
from the contented cooing she emitted and owlish gaze
she allowed to rove over his face, it seemed exactly
where she wanted to be.

Emmaline had to admit that Miss Clarise and Big
Daddy were right. It really was odd how much the
baby looked like Johnny. They shared the same dark
hair, the same dimples deeply imbedded at the corners
of the same finely chiseled lips and the same slight
dip in the same perfectly sculpted nose.

They seemed to recognize each other. Already soul mates, and the baby was not yet more than several hours old.

Though he relinquished her long enough to have her Apgar scores taken, and to be reasonably cleaned and swaddled, the moment the nurses were done, the beaming Johnny scooped her back into his arms.

"Hey, Rosebud!" he crooned, holding her tightly against his chest. "Remember me? I'm the one whose been talkin' to you all this time. Remember? The one whose gonna teach you to ride the horsey? Yeah. You remember. I can see."

Even the nurse who'd come to take the baby down the hall for some routine tests had been out of luck. Johnny had insisted on taking her for the tests himself. And when another poor nurse had moved to prick her tiny foot and capture a few drops of blood, Johnny had pretty much come unhinged. Of course, once the woman had made him understand that this was standard procedure, and in the baby's best interest, he'd consented.

However, he'd held and comforted the baby.

When Emmaline's parents had arrived on the scene, Johnny had turned the baby over to Mrs. Arthur with great reluctance. But not without a litany of instruction.

"Watch her head. Her neck is weak. Hold her like this. Right. Like that. That's the best way, actually. And don't forget the soft spot." He hovered at his mother-in-law's side, fussing until Mrs. Arthur shooed him off.

"Johnny, dear, Emmaline may be an only child, but I do remember a thing or two about holding a baby."

Clucking and tsking, she'd gently scolded, pleased with his obvious adoration of the baby.

As the family crowded around Mrs. Arthur and Rosanne, Johnny found himself at loose ends. Then, seeming to suddenly remember Emmaline, moved to her side wearing a contrite expression.

"Hey, sweetheart." He stroked her hair away from her face. "I didn't mean to ignore you."

"It's okay."

It really was. This whole situation could have turned out so differently without Johnny Brubaker. She would be forever grateful to him for his support and friendship on this day.

"No, no." A self-deprecating grin stole across his face. "It's just that when I saw her, it really hit me. She's a real person." He glanced over his shoulder at his family. "And not just to me, but to them."

"They seem to like her."

"Not as much as I do."

Emmaline chuckled. "So I noticed."

"Am I hogging her?"

"People expect daddies to hog their little girls."

A plethora of emotion crossed his face, and he gazed at her with sudden unshed tears brimming in his eyes.

"Isn't she beautiful?" She had to choke the words out around the lump in her throat.

"Yes. But no more so than you."

Emmaline's breath caught as she looked up at him. When he said things like that, with such an earnest look on his face, she was tempted to believe him. Somehow Johnny Brubaker made her feel truly beautiful. Even wiped out as she was from exhaustion and painkillers. Reaching up, she cupped his whisker-roughened cheek in her hand. He was so incredibly sweet. She was going to miss him something fierce after she and Rosanne moved out. A stab of melancholy threatened to rend her heart in two. How would she survive without him? Rosanne's birth was the first bittersweet signal of the end of their relationship.

Eyes flashing, his gaze burned into hers. Slowly he lowered his head, and his lips captured hers in a kiss so tender, so filled with wonder, Emmaline feared she'd expire right there. His rough, day-old beard rasped against her cheek as he kissed and nuzzled her, telling her without words the feelings of the awe this day had inspired.

With all her heart Emmaline wished that this poignant tableau composed of a loving couple sharing their newborn with family were real. Not some hoax they'd devised to bail each other out of a jam.

As Johnny continued kissing her, Emmaline heard Big Daddy crow. "That baby's a Brubaker, all right. A Brubaker, through and through."

# Chapter Eleven

Emmaline had an incredible sense of déjà vu as she watched the bride and groom whirl around the hotel's ballroom floor. It had been one year ago, nearly to the day, that she'd watched Nora and her new husband share their first dance as a married couple.

Today, at this wedding reception, the bride was no less radiant. The groom no less besotted. Emmaline envied them their mutual adoration and undying love. Felicity Lowenstone was a lucky woman. Finding true love and marriage, so soon after breaking off her engagement was a miracle that many women don't experience.

Emmaline seriously doubted that she would be so fortunate when her time came to break up with Johnny. Squeezing her eyes tightly shut, she swallowed against the tightness in her throat. Her own breakup with her husband was imminent. Try as she might to savor each moment, the sands of time were slipping through the hourglass, leaving her feeling more helpless and lonely than she'd ever felt in her life. Misty-eyed, she watched Felicity with an unaccustomed stab of envy, as the happy bride floated around the room, her head tossed back with laughter and carefree abandon.

When the invitation to Felicity's grand wedding had come in the mail, both she and Johnny had been surprised and happy for the betrothed couple. The enclosed personal note from Felicity had forgiven and forgotten and all but thanked Emmaline for the chance to meet and marry her "true" love, millionaire banker Gunther Howard Zimmerman, III. So, in a fit of love-inspired benevolence, Felicity had invited the entire Brubaker clan to witness her nuptials.

And even Emmaline, who did not set stock in physical appearance, had to admit that, although good old, chubby, balding Gunther couldn't hold a candle to Johnny in the looks department, Felicity seemed genuinely mad over him, and vice versa.

As Emmaline's gaze traveled around the familiar ballroom, she suddenly realized she was standing in almost the exact same spot that she'd been the night Ronny Shumacher—if that was indeed his name—had asked her to dance at Nora's wedding.

The memories never ceased to rattle her. Shivering with chagrin, she wrapped her arms around her middle and cast her gaze about, searching the room for Johnny. She'd lost him in the social milieu a half hour ago.

The giant ballroom was overflowing with happy well-wishers. Music, played by a live symphony orchestra filled the air, straining at the walls and drifting out into the hotel's lavish lobby. Mingling guests of the bride and groom chatted as best they could above the din, and the elegant sounds of crystal and silver made a harmonious underscore.

A smile tugged at Emmaline's lips as she finally spotted Johnny. He beamed with pride as he cradled two-month-old Rosanne against his chest. Her tiny, lacy bottom peeped out from beneath the pink flounces of her ruffly dress. Johnny was making small talk with Felicity's mother who—a gentle smile gracing her lips—listened to Johnny while she stroked Rosanne's downy head. Emmaline was glad to see that at least someone was getting the happy-ever-after ending that they deserved.

Inhaling deeply, Emmaline steadied herself against a cool marble pillar and tried to blow away the remorse she felt building in the pit of her stomach. So much had changed in her life since she was here last. Unfortunately the changes were only beginning. In two short weeks she and Johnny would announce their plans to divorce. And once again she would be single.

Beads of sweat dotted her forehead, and she was suddenly assailed with a feeling of nausea that rivaled morning sickness. She rummaged through her purse, found a tissue and dabbed at her temples. The mere thought of life without Johnny had her sick with sorrow. In the week that would follow their announcement, she and Rosanne would move into their own apartment and begin their life together. Soon all the prearranged papers would be signed and filed. Their agreement would be finalized, the deal would be done. Their life as a married couple would be over.

Ironically, Felicity's marital life would be just beginning.

No use standing here feeling sorry for herself, she decided in a brave attempt to toss off her funk. She pushed away from the pillar that had been holding her up and she set out to join her husband and daughter and enjoy what was left of Felicity's reception. There was plenty of time to wallow in regret later.

As she wended her way through the throng toward the spot she hoped Johnny was still standing in, Emmaline spotted his profile over on the far side of the room and set out after him. Seemed he and Rosanne were making the rounds. Johnny couldn't resist bending the ears of anyone who would listen about the brilliance of his fine daughter.

After a few minutes of serious maneuvering through the masses, Emmaline made it to Johnny's side and paused. Funny. He wasn't holding the baby. How odd. Johnny never let anyone hold the baby. Not even his own mother. Odder still was the fact that he'd removed his jacket and appeared to be flirting with a beautiful young woman who Emmaline had never seen before. However, before a pang of jealous alarm could register, Emmaline froze.

This man was not Johnny Brubaker.

Recoiling in recognition, she took a shaky step back, her heart leaping into her throat and cutting off her air supply.

It couldn't be.

But it was.

This man was Ronny Shumacher.

Head reeling, Emmaline could only stare in morbid fascination at the man who, less than a year ago, had changed her life irrevocably. For a long moment, Emmaline simply watched as this smooth operator stalked his quarry, switching tactics when his advances were not immediately accepted.

Luckily, she noted, this woman seemed to have

more street sense than Emmaline had had a year ago. After politely extricating herself from Ronny's clutches, the young woman moved off into the crowd to the safety of her friends.

Ronny did not seem fazed in the least. As his eyes, like heat-seeking missiles, scanned the ballroom for another unsuspecting target, Emmaline debated whether or not to approach him. For nearly a year now, she'd fantasized about this moment. What she would do. What she would say.

Well-rehearsed dialogue comprised of everything from scathing rebukes to Felicity-like gratitude for opening her life to true love flashed through her mind, leaving her in a quivering quandary.

Gathering her courage before she was tempted to turn tail and bolt, Emmaline squared her shoulders, took a deep breath and prepared to face Ronny again for the first time in a year. Deep in her heart she knew that there was no way she could be this close to her baby's father without at least giving him a chance to accept or reject his biological daughter. It was only fair to Rosanne. No matter how she personally felt about the blankety-blank jerk.

As Emmaline stepped into his field of vision it was clear that he did not recognize her and thought she was on the prowl. Immediately, she was greeted with the lecherous smile that had haunted her dreams these many months. With an incredible effort she forced herself to shake off her qualms and as calmly as she could, returned his smile.

"Hello." She noted with a certain amount of pride that her voice only shook a little.

Ronny's handsome face lit up like the Christmas

tree at Rockefeller Plaza, and his gaze sized her up as a possible conquest.

Emmaline's stomach churned with disgust.

Ronny cocked a brow and bestowed her with a lopsided grin. "Why, hello there."

The deep timbre of his smooth, purring tones grated on her nerves, bringing back vivid memories that threatened to shrivel her self-esteem even now. How could she ever have fallen for this...this...snake oil salesman?

With deliberate intimacy, Ronny hung a casual arm on the wall and, leaning toward her, held out his free hand. "Ronald Rosencrantz. Nice to meet you."

"Rosencrantz?" Emmaline willed her racing pulse to slow and forced herself to take his hand. "You must not be from around here."

Ronny lifted a shoulder. "Only when I need to be. You a friend of the bride or the groom?"

"The bride." Though thoroughly revolted by his demeanor, Emmaline couldn't contain her curiosity. "You?"

Ronny laughed conspiratorially. "Neither. I travel a lot on business. Whenever I hear loud music coming from a hotel ballroom, I figure, Ronny old boy, there's a party in there that needs you. It's a great way to meet friends, if you know what I mean." He arched a roguish brow.

"Yes, as a matter of fact, I do know." Emmaline's blood began to boil, and in that instant the fear that she'd carried with her for over a year began to dissipate.

Delighted, he leaned closer. "You do?"

"Oh, yes." Affecting a flirtatious smile, she angled

her head and smiled in what she hoped was a coquettish fashion. "In fact, we've met before."

"We have?" Brow wrinkled, Ronny scanned his memory. "Now that can't be, cuz I'd sure remember a beautiful woman like you."

"Be that as it may, I'm sure we've met. In fact, it was right here in this very room, just about a year ago."

"Really?"

"Uh-huh. You'd brought some friends and they'd made a little wager with you. Something about seducing the town virgin."

Ronny stared at her, a blank look on his face. Clearly, he still wasn't associating Emmaline Brubaker with Emmaline Arthur. She couldn't blame him his inability to see. She almost didn't recognize herself, these days.

"I'm not sure I follow…"

Emmaline's nod was sympathetic, despite her urge to punch him in the face. "Allow me to clarify. I'm the pitifully dull and uninteresting spinster that could never satisfy a man. Remember? We were briefly engaged? For all of six or seven hours, as I recall. I was to become Mrs. Ronny Shumacher that very morning. Although I guess my name would be Rosencrantz? Or perhaps your real name is—" she smiled sweetly "—Ron Juan?"

His voice was barely above a whisper, Ronny blanched. "That was you?"

"Uh-huh. Oh, but don't worry, I'm not at all upset with the way things turned out."

"You're not?"

"No, no, no. You see, I'm a mother and happy homemaker now."

Relieved, Ronny grinned, rallying. "Well, I must say it agrees with you. You're looking mighty fine."

"Thank you. I owe much of my happiness today to you."

With a tilt of his chin, Ronny once again became the arrogant gigolo who'd seduced her last year at this time. "And why is that?"

"Why, because of our daughter."

Ronny's beguiling smile faded. "Come again?"

"Our baby daughter. Mine—" she looked him right in the eye, "—and yours." Emmaline felt a small thrill at his look of panic. "Yes, I found out I was pregnant shortly after our encounter."

Ronny's face twisted into a hard, skeptical knot. "What? What are you talking about? Baby? What baby?"

"I didn't mention the baby? Oh, dear. My mistake. But you made it kind of tough with your revolving last name."

"Hey, lady..." Ronny's nervous laughter rang hollow. "Just because you had a baby doesn't make it mine." His upper lip curled, and his voice grew more glacial with each word as he scrutinized her face. "What do you want from me, anyway?"

"Oh, the baby is yours, all right. I was the town virgin, remember? Until I ran into you, in any event." Emmaline lifted her shoulders in a philosophical shrug.

So focused on Ronny was she, Emmaline did not notice that Johnny had moved up behind her, the babbling and cooing Rosanne nestled happily in the crook of his arm. Remaining covert in his stance just beyond one of Felicity's extravagant floral displays, Johnny rocked and whispered to the baby. Fascinated, he

watched and listened to Emmaline's conversation with
the man who could have passed for his brother.

"Anyway," he heard Emmaline say, "you asked
what I want. Well now, that's a very good question.
One perhaps I should be asking you. You have a
daughter. Would you like a relationship with her? And
if so, to what degree? I presume you travel too much
to really be much of a hands-on kind of daddy—"

Ducking farther behind the flowers, Johnny tightened his grip on the baby, then murmured his apology
when she squeaked in protest.

Ronny's eyes were hard. Calculating. "Listen, lady,
I don't know what kind of game you're playing
here—"

"Oh, I assure you, it's no game. You are a fath—"

"Prove it!" His words fired from between the hard
line of his lips like arrows from an archer's bow.
"How do I know you're not lying? You get yourself
knocked up and try to pin the blame on me. Well, I'm
not go—"

Johnny strained toward the floral arrangement that
concealed him, struggling to hear and see without being detected.

Her nod curt, Emmaline cut Ronny off. "I understand. You wish to have no part in your daughter's
life."

It was all Johnny could do to keep his mouth shut
and his fists wrapped tightly around the baby as Ronny
exploded with a round of curses that could easily wilt
the flowers behind which he hid.

Red-faced and the veins in his neck bulging, Ronny
took a menacing step toward Emmaline. His voice was
as hard and cold as steel. "You'll stay away from me,

lady, if you know what's good for you.'' Barely re-strained fury glittered in his eyes.

"Fine. I've done my part. I have informed you of the truth and you reject it.'' Emmaline drew herself up, clearly willing her flagging courage to sustain her for one more minute. "And I can't say that I'm sorry. It is obvious that you are not the kind of man I want involved my little girl's life. Ever. No amount of child support or knowledge of a biological father would be worth having you around. So you don't need to worry, Ronny Shumacher or Rosencrantz or whoever you are.''

Tears pooled at her lashes and Emmaline's eyes were suspiciously bright. Her chin quivered as she stood tall and looked Ronny in the eyes. "Luckily for her, she already has a father figure. Someone who loves her. Someone who would move heaven and earth to keep her happy and safe. Someone wonderful and sweet and loving and kind. Attributes you wouldn't know about, though, isn't that right, Ronny?''

Johnny's throat slammed shut with emotion as Emmaline spoke.

"Until this moment I didn't realize just how very, very lucky she is. How very lucky *I* am, to have this man in our lives. What an amazing contrast. You would not give your own flesh and blood the time of day, yet he is willing to give this baby not only his name, but his love and support, as well. No wonder she loves him so much.'' Emmaline closed her eyes and smiled a peace-filled smile. "No wonder *I* do. He is a real father. Something you could never be.''

His blood suddenly coursing loudly through his ears, Johnny wondered if he'd heard correctly. Had

Emmaline just admitted that she loved him? Jostling Rosanne in his arms, he attempted to quiet her impatient fussing so that he could hear.

"You know—" Emmaline looked at Ronny and shook her head "—I've been such a fool, withholding my affection from a certain man. But that's all changing, starting now. I'm going to go tell my baby's real father how much I love and appreciate him. So, if you'll excuse me…"

With a snort of derision, Ronny took a step back and shook his head. "You're crazy, lady. Nuts."

Emmaline nodded. "I was. But not anymore. Now that we've had our little conversation, I'm going to be on my way. Hopefully you and I will never cross paths again."

"Count on it," Ronny spat over his shoulder, and without a departing glance stalked out of the ballroom.

As Johnny moved up next to her—the baby still cradled football-style in the crook of his arm—his gaze followed Emmaline's to Ronny's retreating form.

"Hi." He kept his voice low so as not to startle her.

"Hi." Her response was breathy, her smile tremulous as she glanced up at him.

"How are you doing?"

"Fine. Wonderful, actually. Better than I have for a long, long time."

"Me, too." Johnny felt his heart beat ever faster as he handed the baby to Emmaline. "Listen, could you hold her for a little while? I have some business to attend to. I'll only be gone for a second."

Emmaline nodded. "Sure. But Johnny? If you have a moment I have something I need to talk to you about. It's…important."

"No problem. I promise, this won't take more than a second."

"Okay."

Johnny smiled and gave the side of her temple a quick kiss. "Great. I'll be back before you can miss me."

True to his word Johnny returned quickly. Far too quickly. So quickly in fact, that Emmaline had not had time to really formulate what she wanted to say. How on earth would she admit to her business partner that she'd fallen in love with him? She needed more time. She wanted to do it right. To avoid the potential for error. That was how Emmaline did everything. Slowly. Methodically. With great forethought. She couldn't risk making another colossal mistake, the way she had with Ronny. Head spinning, she followed as Johnny ushered her to an empty table in the corner.

Though afternoon was slipping into evening, Felicity's reception showed no signs of slowing down. As Emmaline and Johnny settled into their seats, baby Rosanne slept peacefully in Johnny's arms, content in the knowledge that she was well cared for and very much loved. By both of her parents.

Unable to stand the tension any longer, Emmaline decided to damn the torpedoes and try to express her deepest and most secret feelings to her husband.

"Uh, Johnny?" Her gaze flickered to his, then away, then back again. "There's something I need to talk to you about." She sagged back into her chair and watched as he made himself comfortable in his own seat.

"Shoot," he urged, then leaned back, the baby asleep on his shoulder.

Emmaline took a deep breath. "Well, just a few minutes ago I ran into Rosanne's..." She paused and frowned. Johnny was Rosanne's father. Not Ronny. "I, uh, ran into Ronny Shumacher."

"Rosanne's father?"

"Her...biological father, yes."

He lifted his chin and peered at her over the baby.

Emmaline couldn't tell what he was thinking, and it rattled her. Lifting the hem of the tablecloth, she twisted it between her fingers.

"I thought Ronny Shumacher was his name. Today, he told me it was Rosencrantz. I'm not really sure what his name is, actually."

"He told me it was Chapman."

Emmaline stared at him not quite comprehending. "You spoke to Ronny?"

"Uh-huh."

"My Ronny?"

"Is he your Ronny?" His tone was dry.

Emmaline grimaced. "You know what I mean."

A grin forked the corners of Johnny's eyes. "Yes, I know what you mean."

"How did you know it was him?"

"I have my ways."

Eyes narrowed, Emmaline leaned forward. "When did you talk to him?"

"Just now. Out in the hotel parking lot."

"What were you doing out there?"

"Just checking up on our boy."

"And he told you his name was Chapman?"

"Yep." Johnny stretched and yawned. "Just before I punched him out."

Emmaline's jaw fell open and her laughter was incredulous. "You...what? Why?"

"Didn't like the looks of him."

"But you look just like him!"

"Not anymore. He's sportin' a couple of shiners that will take weeks to go away."

Emmaline could scarcely believe what she was hearing. "So you really knew that he was Rosanne's biological father?"

"Yep."

"But how?" She gripped his hand. "C'mon. Tell me."

"I...accidentally overheard you two talking."

Her mouth suddenly dry, Emmaline attempted to swallow. "What—" she cleared her throat "—um, what exactly did you hear?" Had he heard her say that she loved him? Her pulse hammered relentlessly.

"Not much. Just enough to know that he needed a lesson in how to treat a woman."

"Oh." So, he probably hadn't heard the part about her undying love. She wondered how she was going to slip that little tidbit into this conversation.

"It would seem that the big bad wolf was already in the process of leading another little lamb off to slaughter."

Emmaline sighed. "Why doesn't that surprise me?"

Shifting the baby in his arms, Johnny looked at her with poignant regret. "I couldn't be there when he was up to no good with you last year. I'd give anything to roll back the clock, go to Nora and Chuck's wedding and deck him before he hurt you. But, that's twenty-twenty hindsight. And—" tucking his chin, his gaze on the peacefully snoozing Rosanne, his expression fierce in its need to protect "—we wouldn't have her. So, tonight, while I had the opportunity, I thought I'd get in a couple of licks, for old-times' sake. 'Just desserts' and all that.''

His sweet grin was so tender and endearing her eyes suddenly filled with tears. He cared that much about her? Raw emotion crowded into her throat, preventing her from speaking.

"I think I managed to convince Mr. Shumacher-Rosencrantz-Chapman-Scumbag that if I ever caught his face in these parts again, I'd be there to welcome him personally. That seemed to shake him up.''

Emmaline dabbed at her eyes with the hem of the tablecloth. "Thank you." Her voice was barely above a whisper. "For caring enough for us to do that.''

He shrugged off her gratitude. "As sad and pathetic as his attitude toward the baby is, I have to admit, I'm glad he doesn't want anything to do with her. As far as I'm concerned, she's my daughter, and that's how I want it to stay.''

Emmaline felt a jolt of hope spring to life in her heart. "Me, too.''

"He doesn't deserve either of you.''

"Oh, Johnny." She blubbered into the tablecloth.

An expression of yearning flashed into his eyes, and it was clear the words he was about to speak meant a great deal to him. "I want you to know that I'll always be there for you and Rosanne, no matter what.''

"I know.''

*No matter what.*

The words were a dismal reminder that he still expected to divorce and that soon they would be going their separate ways. Emmaline couldn't stand to let the conversation turn toward the dissolution of their union and so, still needing time to figure out how to confess her love to him, she used a diversionary tactic.

"Felicity made a beautiful bride."

"Not half as beautiful as you did."

Emmaline's sigh was ragged as she shook her head in disbelief and dabbed at the tears that streamed down her cheeks.

"It's true, Emmaline. You were a sight for sore eyes. Still are."

"Shut up." She hiccuped and giggled, not believing, but touched by his earnest expression.

"They will be leaving on their honeymoon soon." He tossed this casual remark out, but watched intently from hooded eyes for her reaction.

"I'm a little jealous," she confessed, bashfully. "That's one thing we never got to do."

"There are a lot of things we've never done."

"Well, I suppose it's too late now."

"It doesn't have to be...."

"What do you mean?"

"You could tell me that you love me. That's one thing you haven't done."

"But..." Emmaline's mouth went suddenly dry. "That's because it wasn't part of the deal."

"True, and it wasn't part of the deal for me to fall madly in love with you. But I managed to do that, anyway."

What? Her eyes wide with shock, Emmaline could only stare. Was he saying what she thought he was saying?

"Uh," she touched her tongue to her lips. "I don't think that I...you know...heard you correctly. Would you mind repeating what you...uh, just said, there?"

Deep dimples bracketed Johnny's smiling lips. "What? The part about the things we've never done, or the part about me falling in love with you?"

"You did?" Leaning forward, she peered into his face. "You fell in love with me?"

Johnny sighed. "Emmaline Brubaker, until the day of our wedding, and I kissed you that first time, I had no idea what love was. And even then, I was reluctant to admit the power you held over me. I fought it the best I could, but it was futile. I'm a goner. You are everything I've ever wanted in a woman. Smart, talented, funny. You are incredibly beautiful. Inside and out."

Twisting in her seat, Emmaline looked up at him, barely able to believe. Eyes sparkling, she searched his face for the truth.

"You...love me?"

"With all my heart." The solemn tone of his voice and the sincerity in his eyes had her pulse churning. "Except," he amended with a grin of fatherly pride, "for the part of my heart that I've given to her." He nuzzled the sleeping baby. "But, that's another story."

"Oh, Johnny." The tension in Emmaline's face eased and tears of joy sprang into her eyes. "I love you, too. So very, very much."

She cupped his jawline in her hands, drew him forward and touched her lips to his. His whiskers rasped pleasantly against her smooth skin as he leaned over her and deepened the kiss. A long minute later Rosanne voiced her dismay at being crushed between their bodies, and, chuckling, Johnny came up for air. His free hand was tangled in Emmaline's hair, and his lips brushed hers as he spoke.

"Say you'll marry me." He kissed her again, hard.

"We're already married." She pulled him back for another.

"Say we'll stay married." His lips moved to her jaw and then to the sensitive point behind her ear where her pulse raged. "Say the business deal is off. Say you'll be my wife and Rosanne will be my daughter."

"Forever?" She breathed the word against his mouth, nipping playfully at his lower lip with her teeth.

"And ever." Johnny nuzzled her nose with the tip of his. "You know, that Ronny What's-His-Face is a real fool."

"Why is that?"

"Well, for one thing, for a dull and uninteresting spinster, you're doing a pretty good job of setting me on fire, right about now."

Emmaline giggled and wound her arms up around his shoulders, embracing him and the baby at the same time. As she spoke, her murmured words were ragged against his cheek. "Um. And, I think the fire is spreading."

He paused and looked deeply into her eyes. "In that case, may I suggest that tonight we let the honeymoon begin?"

Breath whooshing from her lungs, Emmaline was giddy with anticipation as she replied. "By all means."

"I'm going to have mom baby-sit tonight, okay?"

"You mean you actually trust someone else to take care of Rosanne?" She couldn't resist teasing him.

His grin was sheepish. "Well, she is her grandmother. And, it's just for the evening. A minihoneymoon. We can plan a longer one later." He regarded her lazily.

"Ah. Good thinking." Mock consternation knit her

brows. "A minihoneymoon. It's not the around-the-world extravaganza Felicity had planned by any stretch."

"Who cares?"

"Then you're not disappointed?"

He snorted. "Hardly."

Feeling punch-drunk with the heady power of his love, Emmaline's laughter burbled against his mouth. "Me, neither."

Johnny groaned. "In fact, I have an idea, Mrs. Brubaker."

"Yes?" Emmaline loved the sound of her name on his lips.

"When we get home, the first thing I want to do is..."

"Ye-e-e-e-s?" Emmaline giggled.

"Get rid of that stupid air mattress."

"And what's the second thing you want to do?"

"Dig out some of that wacky underwear Patsy gave us for our first honeymoon."

Emmaline inhaled and, voice high with excitement, whispered against his chin. "And the third thing?"

"Get started on a little brother for Rosanne."

A flash of gooseflesh raced up her spine. "Oh, my. I think that's the best idea I've heard all year."

\* \* \* \* \*

*Watch for more Brubakers—this time from a whole new branch of the family— as* THE BRUBAKER BRIDES *series continues soon from Silhouette Romance.*

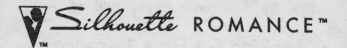

# *Silhouette* ROMANCE™

Join *Silhouette Romance*
as more couples experience
the joy only babies
can bring!

**Bundles of Joy**

**September 1999**
**THE BABY BOND**
**by Lilian Darcy (SR #1390)**

Tom Callahan a daddy? Impossible! Yet that was before Julie Gregory showed up with the shocking news that she carried his child. Now the father-to-be knew marriage was the answer!

**October 1999**
**BABY, YOU'RE MINE**
**by Lindsay Longford (SR #1396)**

Marriage was the *last* thing on Murphy Jones's mind when he invited beautiful—and pregnant—Phoebe McAllister to stay with him. But then she and her newborn bundle filled his house with laughter...and had bachelor Murphy rethinking his no-strings lifestyle....

### And in December 1999, popular author
# MARIE FERRARELLA
### brings you
## THE BABY BENEATH THE MISTLETOE (SR #1408)

Available at your favorite retail outlet.

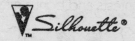
*Silhouette*®

Of all the unforgettable families created by
#1 *New York Times* bestselling author

# NORA ROBERTS

the Donovans are the most extraordinary. For, along with
their irresistible appeal, they've inherited some rather
remarkable gifts from their Celtic ancestors.

*Coming in November 1999*

## THE DONOVAN LEGACY

3 full-length novels in one special volume:

**CAPTIVATED:** Hardheaded skeptic Nash Kirkland has *always*
kept his feelings in check, until he falls under the bewitching
spell of mysterious Morgana Donovan.

**ENTRANCED:** Desperate to find a missing child, detective
Mary Ellen Sutherland dubiously enlists beguiling
Sebastian Donovan's aid and discovers his uncommon abilities
include a talent for seduction.

**CHARMED:** Enigmatic healer Anastasia Donovan would do
anything to save the life of handsome Boone Sawyer's
daughter, even if it means revealing her secret to the man
who'd stolen her heart.

*Also in November 1999 from Silhouette Intimate Moments*

## ENCHANTED

Lovely, guileless Rowan Murray is drawn to darkly enigmatic
Liam Donovan with a power she's never imagined possible. But
before Liam can give Rowan his love, he must first reveal to
her his incredible secret.

### ▼ *Silhouette*®
™

Available at your favorite retail outlet.

# Don't miss Silhouette's newest cross-line promotion,

*Four royal sisters find their own Prince Charmings as they embark on separate journeys to find their missing brother, the Crown Prince!*

The search begins in October 1999 and continues through February 2000:

On sale October 1999: **A ROYAL BABY ON THE WAY** by award-winning author **Susan Mallery** (Special Edition)

On sale November 1999: **UNDERCOVER PRINCESS** by bestselling author **Suzanne Brockmann** (Intimate Moments)

On sale December 1999: **THE PRINCESS'S WHITE KNIGHT** by popular author **Carla Cassidy** (Romance)

On sale January 2000: **THE PREGNANT PRINCESS** by rising star **Anne Marie Winston** (Desire)

On sale February 2000: **MAN...MERCENARY...MONARCH** by top-notch talent **Joan Elliott Pickart** (Special Edition)

## ROYALLY WED
### Only in—
## SILHOUETTE BOOKS

Available at your favorite retail outlet.

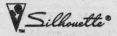

Visit us at www.romance.net

SSERW

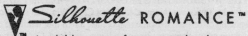

# Silhouette
# ™ ROMANCE™

## COMING NEXT MONTH

**#1408 THE BABY BENEATH THE MISTLETOE—Marie Ferrarella**
*Bundles of Joy*
Natural-born nurturer Michelle Rozanski wasn't about to let Tony Marino face instant fatherhood alone. Even if Tony could be gruffer than a hibernating bear, he'd made a place in his home—and heart—for an abandoned child. And now if Michelle had her way, they'd *never* face parenthood alone!

**#1409 EXPECTING AT CHRISTMAS—Charlotte Maclay**
When his butler was away, the *last* replacement millionaire Griffin Jones expected was eight-months-pregnant Loretta Santana. Yet somehow she'd charmed him into hiring her. And now this confirmed bachelor found himself falling for Loretta...and her Christmas-baby-on-the-way....

**#1410 EMMA AND THE EARL—Elizabeth Harbison**
*Cinderella Brides*
She thought she'd outgrown dreams of happily-ever-after, yet when American Emma Lawrence found herself a guest of Earl Brice Palliser's lavish estate, he seemed her very own Prince Charming come to life. But was there a place in Brice's noble heart for plain Emma?

**#1411 A DIAMOND FOR KATE—Moyra Tarling**
The moment devastatingly handsome Dr. Marshall Diamond entered the hospital, nurse Kate Turner recognized him as the man she'd secretly loved as a child. But could Kate convince him that the girl from his past was now a woman he could trust...forever?

**#1412 THE MAN, THE RING, THE WEDDING—Patricia Thayer**
*With These Rings*
Tall, dark and *rich* John Rossi was cozying up to innocent Angelina Covelli for one reason—revenge. But old family feuds weren't sweet enough to keep the sexy CEO fixed on his goal. His mind—and heart—kept steering him to Angelina...and rings...and weddings!

**#1413 THE MILLIONAIRE'S PROPOSITION—Natalie Patrick**
Waitress Becky Taylor was tempted to accept Clark Winstead's proposal. It was an enticing offer—a handsome millionaire, a rich life, family. If only it wasn't lacking a few elements...like a wedding...and love. Good thing Becky was planning to do a little enticing of her own....

CMN1199